Not Even A Mouse

MariaLisa deMora

Edited by Hot Tree Editing

Copyright © 2017 MariaLisa deMora

First Published 2017

ISBN 13: 978-1-946738-10-3

DEDICATION

Thank you to my huge, extended, and still
growing family for reminding me that—trite as it
sounds—love truly is love.

CONTENTS

ACKNOWLEDGMENTS

Every story is magic. They all begin with an idle thought. If allowed time to mature, if cultivated, that thought can become an idea. If fed and carefully tended, that idea can grow until it exceeds the bounds of anything the idle thought ever dreamed of becoming.

This story began with an idle thought. The summer I was five-years-old, a beloved small-town country doctor removed my chronically-infected tonsils and adenoids. The surgery went well. Then, I nearly died a week later when I hemorrhaged from the site, gushing blood from my carotid artery. That was the second time in my life I almost died.

Summer being construction season in East Texas, our county highway was being resurfaced, and long sections of it were closed for extended periods of time so the heavy equipment could do their work. Refusing to wait, my mother drove our 1964 Dodge Polara—I know the model because I've remembered the novelty of its push-button automatic transmission—through the ditch for a considerable distance to get us around the construction zone.

When we arrived at the local hospital, the doctor met us in the lobby and the doctor whisked me away from my mother. I'd like to draw you a picture of how pale he was in response to the dire situation, but the honest thing is I don't remember what he looked like, just the terrified expression on my mom's face. I do remember the sound his feet made as he hurried up the rubber-covered incline leading to the second floor—slap, slap,

slap. It was a head-bobbing awkward run which I am certain he felt in his bones for days following, as he wasn't a young man. The cauterization was a success—obviously, as I'm still here—but...let's just say traumatic is a too-frail word for the rushed procedure used to stop the bleeding on a completely conscious little girl.

So, my idle thought was: What if a little girl went through what I did, but the story's focus was on the parent? Not the scene from my remembered child's point of view, but how it was for my mother to sit in that lobby, the shoulder of her shirt covered in drying blood, impatiently waiting to learn if her life would be the same at the end of the day. My dad was at work in Longview, and I believe it was that night before she was able to get word to him of what happened. That meant it was possible she sat alone for hours.

Then, my next idle thought was: What if she could call on someone for support, but in doing so irrevocably change their lives in some way?

In a flash, Myron raised his hand, and it was off to the writing-races, because I knew where we were headed, and I have to say...I like where we got to with this story. I hope you enjoy it, too.

Remember, love comes in all sorts of packages. We just need to be brave enough to begin the unwrapping process. If we do that, and trust our hearts, then just like idle thoughts turning into stories, magic will happen. Promise.

Woofully yours,
~ML

Where things began

"Boy, you wanna explain what that school principal sent this paper home for?"

No, fourteen-year-old Ronnie absolutely did not want to explain why the school wanted to have a parent-teacher conference. There were few things he was certain of these days, but explaining to Mr. Younger what the teacher had seen today was a definite no. He stood and tried not to fidget, gaze resolutely angled towards the floor, knowing from experience it was the only way to get through the next few minutes without catching holy heck.

"Boy?" The tone of the single word question had changed, dropping an octave, growing a rough and jagged edge to the sound. Ronnie knew better than to even shake his head, because that would be an admission of something, which would open the door for the rest.

Alan's voice slithered through his head, repeating the same entreaty he'd spouted since Monday. *"You wanna look at the pictures, you gotta do what they show."* Alan had stolen one of his daddy's dirty magazines, no big deal, something he'd done before with no repercussions. Ronnie had never understood the draw, but the boys in class would cluster around the older Alan as if he held the Holy Grail, paying a penny per page to look at the crowded pictures of women on the slick sheets of paper.

Monday, though, the magazine Alan brought to school had a special section in the back. Ronnie had gotten only a glimpse as Alan fanned through the pages, teasing his crew, and what he saw left Ronnie standing with his mouth open like he was a stupe. He'd lined up with the other boys, penny in hand, stepping out of line and back in behind the next boy, and the next, until he'd been the last one and they had only a few minutes before recess was over.

"I wanna...see...those." He pointed to the back cover and Alan tipped his head, staring down at him with wide eyes. *"The ones at the back, there."* He held out his hand, one shiny penny lying flat on his palm. Alan smiled, but it wasn't a nice smile. The expression on his face pulled his mouth wide, top lip lifting until he no longer looked like a fifteen-year-old boy, but more like a scary caricature of a man with too-big teeth.

"Meet me back of the gym at lunch." His hand swooped out, fingers plucking the penny from Ronnie's palm. He leaned close and tucked it deep into the front

pocket of Ronnie's pants, fingers digging, rubbing and touching his privates in a way that made his pecker stiffen. "You can look all you want, no charge."

Ronnie had wolfed down his lunch, shoveling the school food into his mouth until it was a wonder he hadn't choked. Alan was a grade ahead of him, and their lunch was earlier. Ronnie was afraid he'd miss the boy and that wasn't something he was going to permit. That single glance of the pictures in that special section had set his heart racing, made all the spit in his mouth dry up.

Empty tray handed through the window to the lunch lady, he'd forced himself to carefully walk to the door and out into the hallway. Turning left, he wound through the maze of halls that led to the back of the activity building, a combination gymnasium and auditorium, blinking at the bright sunshine when he pushed through the door and outside. He looked around in dismay and muttered, "Man," because he didn't see Alan. Lost my chance.

Ronnie turned to head back inside, mind already on his next class period, running through last night's homework when he heard his name.

"Ronnie. Pssst. Over here." Looking around, he saw a hand waving from the tiny alcove next to the gym. When the builders added the gym, decades after the school itself was built, they'd left a tiny strip of space between the sides of the buildings. The area was soggy in rainy season, because the runoff from both roofs turned the ground to mush. It wasn't raining now, and hadn't been, so the dirt was packed. It was where the teachers who smoked went to get away from the kids, where the

upperclassmen went to kiss their girls. And now, it was where Ronnie was going to look at dirty pictures that made his stomach dip and sway.

"Lemme see." He was anxious, already anticipating the moment of unveiling, ready to know for sure if what he'd been feeling was real. "Come on, Alan."

Six inches taller, Alan stood in front of him, magazine folded and tucked under one arm, hands shoved into his pockets. "Won't take your money."

A ball bounced inside the gym, hitting the wall beside Ronnie with such force the smack echoed in the space where they stood. No free rides. He thought of a bumper sticker he'd seen on a semi that touted Ass, Gas, or Grass, nobody rides for free.

There were no free rides in life, and Ronnie knew that truth better than most, because while the Youngers weren't great, they were a far sight better than some of the other fosters he'd lived with in the years since his parents were killed in a car wreck. If Alan didn't want money for Ronnie looking at the magazine, he'd want something else. "Then what?"

"For every page you wanna look at, you gotta do something." The words came out in a rush, tripping over themselves to vacate Alan's mouth.

"Do what?" His brain buzzed with ideas of homework assignments, or carrying lunch trays. Being Alan's toady for a few days might be worth it if what he expected to see was real and not a trick of his imagination.

"What one of the pictures shows." Ronnie stood, mouth open, not breathing. Alan hurried to say, "One picture per page. Whatever one I pick, you gotta do."

Another ball smacked against the inside wall, but Ronnie was so focused on Alan he scarcely heard it, and didn't hear the murmur of voices growing louder in the gym, signaling the lunch period was nearly ended.

"I gotta..." He let his voice trail off. Alan nodded. "Whatever you..." Another truncated sentence, another nod.

It was as if Alan had reached into his head and pulled out the one thing that he wanted more than anything. A reason to try the things that were burning his brain. He opened his mouth but before he could respond, and he might never know what that response might have been, the two-minute bell rang, a shrill warble that held a tinge of warning. Don't be late. Don't be tardy. You'll regret it.

Alan pushed past him and Ronnie felt something smack against his buttocks. Twisting, he saw Alan tuck the magazine back under his arm just before he rounded the corner.

That had been Monday and by the time Tuesday rolled around, Ronnie had a sleepless night under his belt and second thoughts in his head. Wednesday and Thursday, the same, lack of rest coloring deep circles under his eyes.

Then today, Alan had asked a final time, telling him the magazine had to be back in the toolbox in his dad's garage before it got to be beer-thirty. And Ronnie had met him in the alcove. Alan picked a page, folded the magazine so that would be all Ronnie got out of the deal, and had given him two minutes to look his fill.

And look he did, gaze coasting up and down the page, criss-crossing the pictures that were jammed every which way on the printed page. Men. Naked men. Men in some elaborate harness things around their shoulders, and nothing else on their body. Men on beds, asses in the air, one hand back to clutch their cheek so they could show their hole to best effect. There were words too, of a sort, a language Ronnie'd never seen, dots and dashes over and under letters. He looked beyond that to the pictures. Men on their backs, fingers wrapped around their hard peckers. The picture in the center had arrested him, and he spent precious seconds staring at it. Two men, one on his knees with eyes turned up to the face of the one on his feet. He had the man's whole pecker in his mouth, cheeks hollowed out like he was sucking on a straw.

"That one," Alan said, hand appearing over the top of the magazine, finger tapping on the center image. Ronnie didn't look away, kept his gaze on the picture, ignoring Alan's dirty fingernail scoring a line across the man's face. "You'll do it."

"Here?" Ronnie wasn't aware his mouth was still working, thought his tongue had come unhinged in his maw.

"Here." Alan agreed and plucked the magazine back, arranging the pages just so as he closed it, plain brown backing covering the pictures of naked women on the cover. From looking at it now, no one would ever guess it held the reason for Ronnie's heart to be thudding along like it was. Alan's fingers worked at his belt then his pants, and Ronnie watched as he reached inside, hand reappearing, cradling a length of pecker that was impressive. "Put your mouth on it." Alan's fingers gripped the base, splaying out across his crotch, angling his pecker straight out. "Come on, we don't have all day."

Ronnie bent at the waist and hesitated a moment, then slowly swayed forwards that last fraction of an inch and touched his lips to the tip of Alan's pecker, surprised at the dry heat emanating from his flesh.

"Lick it." Alan's directions were easy to follow; simple and to the point, which was good because Ronnie's brain had stopped working a few minutes ago. He pressed his lips to it again, then gave it a lick, as if it were a frosting spoon. "Put it in your mouth."

Ronnie shuffled to the side and angled his head, bending over farther. He reached out and grasped Alan's wrist, holding himself steady as he aimed the pecker at his mouth. "Oh, man," Alan groaned when Ronnie put his lips around the end, memorizing how it felt in his mouth, the weight of it on his lips, how slippery the skin was when he swirled saliva over it with his tongue. He remembered the picture, how the man had been on his knees and Ronnie was attempting to crouch lower when a shocked inhale broke the spell he'd been under.

Straightening, he whirled and looked to see Mrs. Ednell standing there, hand covering her mouth. Alan pushed past him and shoved the math teacher out of his *way, leaving her staggering in his wake. Ronnie lifted a hand and swiped at his lips, surprised they weren't wet.*

"Boy, I find out you've caused trouble at school, you and me will have a chat out in the barn." Mr. Younger hefted his considerable bulk out of his recliner and stalked to where Ronnie stood in the center of the room. His hand landed on Ronnie's shoulder, fingers digging in with brutal strength. "You know what this is, you should just get it over with. You got all weekend to think on it. Come up with the right answer. Be smart. Tell me now, it'll go easier on you."

No it won't.

***

The heavy atmosphere in the cab of the truck was toxic. Their ride back to the foster home taking forever, moments ticking by as slowly as sap pooling on the cut end of a branch.

Ronnie and Alan had stuck to the story they'd come up with in a hurried bathroom conversation that morning. *No, sir. We don't know what Mrs. Ednell thought she saw. Ronnie was just looking at something on the ground.* Ronnie didn't think the principal bought it, and he knew Mr. Younger hadn't believed them for a single second.

Throughout the entire meeting, the parts Ronnie was involved in anyway, Mr. Younger's neck and face gradually had grown a darker and darker red, his blustering words never once defending Ronnie, just working to ensure the school authorities knew he wouldn't stand for such perversion in his house. No siree bob, he'd be taking care of that as soon as he got the boy home.

At least Ronnie knew what he had in front of him.

He thought.

"Pervert, go to the barn." Ronnie jerked and turned to look at the man, seeing only his back as he climbed out of the truck on his side. Not even boy, this time. He slipped out of the truck, careful to close the door gently, knowing slamming it would trigger another round of punishments. He walked to the barn and pushed open the smaller door, going inside and standing for a moment in the soft darkness.

How bad can it be?

A footfall telegraphed Younger's approach and Ronnie turned. He felt lightheaded as blood rushed from his head, fear clotting his brain when he saw the belt in one of Younger's hands, Bible in the other.

"On your knees, pervert. You like it so much, get down there now." Younger didn't even sound mad, so Ronnie stared at him a moment, hoping he'd heard wrong. With a roar, Younger lashed out with the belt, the tail catching Ronnie full across the face in a brutal blow that staggered him. "I said get on your knees, faggot."

Stumbling backwards, feet tripping over each other, his ears buzzing loudly, Ronnie managed to drop to his knees, balancing there by an act of will. His face was numb, and he couldn't stop his eyes from blinking rapidly, vision scored through with stripes of shadow and brilliant light.

Younger's boots scuffed through hay and packed dirt on the barn floor as he stepped closer and Ronnie's gaze came into focus, aimed at the front of the man's pants, where he saw an unmistakable tenting.

The belt came down again and again, each target a new agony as it wrapped over his shoulder, and lashed his ribs, leaving a trail of fire behind every strike. Ronnie cried out as the belt landed unceasing, his whole back screaming in pain.

Younger took another step and stopped in front of Ronnie. "You a little cocksucking faggot, pervert boy?" He bent over and clutched Ronnie's privates, squeezing hard until Ronnie was retching, his hands battering at the tree trunk of an arm connected to the hand that would not let go. "Like sucking cock?" A final squeeze left him blind and mute, mouth open in a silent scream at the explosion of agony that settled in his groin.

Fingers gripped his chin and lifted, squeezed his cheeks in against his teeth until he tasted blood mixing with the bile already in his mouth. "Pervert." He opened his mouth to yell and was choking, gagging around some foul-smelling thing obstructing his airway. Deeper and deeper it pushed, then pulled back and he sucked in air.

Ronnie had found out just how bad it could get.

Business as usual

Thirteen years later

"What the hell are you doing in here, brother?" A sharp kick to the leg of his chair finished jarring Myron awake, and he lifted his head to glare up at the man looming over him. Slate, president of the Rebel Wayfarers MC Fort Wayne chapter, was standing beside the desk, a grin Myron decided to interpret as fond stretched across his face.

He blinked away the remnants of his dream. *That's right, I'm in the Fort.* Ronnie Lyons, known in the club as Myron for reasons he'd kept close to the chest for years, yawned and stretched, rolling his neck.

Slate hadn't been around all day. Myron had ridden in from Chicago mid-morning and immediately started work helping Jase, the club's business manager in the Fort, sort out the end of quarter statements. He had planned to wait for Slate, but gotten engrossed in the minutia of the many businesses. He glanced around. No Jase. *Shit*. Myron cleared his throat and looked down, fingers reaching to straighten the printouts he'd apparently been using as a pillow. His voice was hoarse when he asked, "What do you want? I'm busy."

Slate cackled. "Gettin' busy? This your version of gettin' busy? Fuck, man. This office has seen a lotta action over the years, but that might be the first time anyone's actually slept on that desk. Why didn't you head upstairs? You got the message about the rooms Ruby gave you, right? She hooked you up."

Nodding, Myron folded the pages in half, thumb stroking along the bend to firm the crease. Tidy, just the way he preferred things. "The suite is nice." It was, too. A set of rooms that had been used by a variety of club and family members over the years, the suite included a living space where he could have done this work just as easily. *And without interruptions.* "I was waiting. Heard Gunny's here. I haven't talked to him for eons, thought it might be nice to chat."

"That man is long gone. Headed home to his old lady."

Myron grimaced, scrubbing his jaw with one hand. Two days' worth of stubble made him feel scruffy. "I must have dozed off."

"Fuckin' passed out, you mean." Slate gripped the arms of Myron's chair and scooted it away from the table. "Go to bed, brother. I'm headed home. We can sort everything tomorrow. Ain't nothing so urgent it needs to keep you from your bed, or me from my woman." He walked behind and shoved on the back of the chair, tipping it forwards, and Myron stood in self-defense, stumbling as he found his feet.

"Yeah." As much as Myron hated to leave anything undone, Slate was right. "It can wait." Walking ahead of Slate, he made his way out of the office and through the main room, glancing around to see it full of men, most of which he knew. He slowed with a sigh. He wouldn't mind getting a beer if it were just members, but there was also a plethora of the kind of scantily dressed women who were always hanging around the clubhouse, waiting to be noticed. Not old ladies, but party dolls. *Shit*. "I should—"

A hand landed in the center of his back and steered him firmly towards the stairs. "What you should do is hit the hay, brother. You're dead on your feet, and every man knows it's because you've been working your ass off for the club. No one's gonna fault you for ducking out of Friday night clubhouse drinking. Ain't a party or anything. Sure ain't fuckin' mandatory." Slate's voice was as determined as his grip. "Get some shuteye. We'll finish working the books tomorrow." The hand at his back faltered, and he glanced around to see Slate looking uncertain. His voice was quiet when he continued, "Look, Myron. I know you're fussy about things, but if you want me to send one of the girls up, I can find one to suit you."

Myron scoffed, too tired to stifle the response. *Fussy*. He'd worked damned hard to let it be known he

13

was picky. *Oh, yeah. I'm particular all right.* Aloud, he said, "Nah. I'll just sleep." *And dream.* Each footstep feeling like it was weighted down with cement, he made his way up the stairs.

What he wanted wasn't a party doll. *No, what I'd like to warm my bed is far different.*

He reached the top of the stairs and turned to look around the room again, seeing Slate standing and staring up at him. Myron lifted a hand, a gesture Slate returned before turning towards the bar. But not before Myron saw a look of uncertainty had returned to his friend's face, which for him, was a concerning expression.

Sleep now. Worry later.

***

Thud. Thud. Thud.

Myron sat up and stared across the room. He was in the larger of the two bedrooms, situated directly across the living area from the hallway door. "What the hell?"

Thud. Thud. Thud.

A giggle.

His gut dropped. *Fuck.*

He stood and yanked on his jeans, fastened two buttons and stalked to the door to yank it open. One of the Fort Wayne members stood there, arm wrapped around a woman. She'd lost her top somewhere along the way, bare breasts pressed to the man's chest. Myron spared her a glance then glared at the man's face. Channeling every ounce of intimidation he'd learned from Mason and Slate, he clipped out, "What. The. Fuck?"

"Brute called." *Thank God, it's something to do with the club. Not a pity fuck to be deflected.* He'd sidestepped a lot of well-intentioned efforts through the years. Still listening, Myron walked back and snagged his shirt from the foot of the bed he'd occupied for only a couple of hours. "His woman's at that bar." He grabbed his vest, settling the black leather into place on his shoulders, already knowing where this would end. "You're sober."

"That I am." Myron grabbed his boots and sat on the foot of the bed, watching as the man moved out of view, thankfully taking the woman with him. "Always am." He slid his boots on over his socks and stood, checking his pockets to ensure he had everything he'd need.

It wasn't the first time he'd answered this particular call. There wasn't much hardship in going to a bar and sitting for a couple of hours, especially not if it ensured a brother's woman got home safely.

Downstairs, he lifted a hand and waved at the few remaining members gathered around the bar. "Ride safe," he heard and lifted his chin in mute response.

Always do that, too.

Take me on a ride

Andy

Andrus Kasmouski paused at the back door and leaned his ass against the crashbar, hands filled with trash bags for the dumpster. "Last load," he yelled into the kitchen, "go ahead and leave. I'm finished locking up." He heard an answering call that dwindled down to nothing and knew the cook was already headed out the side door. Grinning, Andy pushed through the door and turned only to stop in surprise. Leaning against the nearby wall, arms folded across his chest, was the biker from inside. *Damn, he looks good.*

After an evening of heated looks and flirty exchanges, Andy had issued the invitation without any real expectation the man would take him up on it. Two hours ago, he'd handed over a drink paired with a scribbled-on napkin featuring a number and time, whispering only, "I get off at two." From the nervous way

16

the guy's gaze had swept the nearby tables, Andy had immediately chalked it up to a nonstarter. The guy was just a curious lookie-loo who wasn't as interested as Andy had initially read him.

Now, even though the biker was the one waiting in the alley, Andy felt something was off. Far from looking relaxed, the man seemed frozen in place. The uncomfortable look on his face suggested his pose was too-casual, a studied posture shouting uncertainty. The silence stretched on while Andy looked him up and down. Finally, as if compelled to speak, the guy blurted, "Hey."

Andy nearly rolled his eyes at the lame greeting. He disposed of the trash and made his way towards the biker. He took his time, moving slowly because he expected the man to bolt at any moment. Hand on one hip, Andy asked, "You waiting on me?" *Please, God, let him be down for this.* Not normally the type to pray for a hookup, but Andy wanted this guy. He'd seemed intelligent and opinionated, willing to debate his points on sports and politics, listening closely when Andy spoke but ready with a rebuttal. Strong and confident, something that was in short supply in Andy's life these days. He found he wanted the kind of release that came from being with someone who might be able to take him outside of his own head for a few minutes.

The where had been up in the air at first. Finances restricted going the hotel route, and Andy didn't normally take his hookups to his home. Not that there were a lot of hookups, but there was too much uncertainty in the world these days to let just anyone know where he lived. But Andy figured the biker wouldn't have any trouble finding out his address if he'd wanted, and something about this guy seemed different.

Trustworthy. Andy focused on that, not the fact the man was in a motorcycle gang.

The tall, quiet man had seemed steady, less frantic to prove himself than so many of the queers who came into the bar. A lot of them were baby gays, expecting if a man like Andy was behind the bar then it would be more LGBTQ welcoming than some of the more redneck places in town. Andy worked hard to make sure the place was safe for those who were trying their freedom, some of them taking their closet-bound training wheels off for the first time. *Like this guy?*

Andy's maybe-date nodded jerkily and reached out, resting one hand palm-first against Andy's chest. He looked surprised at the contact, almost as if his body had acted without his permission. Andy covered the hand, tucking his fingers around to hold it in place, liking the heat and firmness of the touch. *Oh, yeah. I can work with this guy.*

The temperature was unexpectedly balmy, shirt-sleeve comfortable for a late fall night, the air warm as bathwater around them. Andy looked around and found the angular shadow he'd expected, up near the building where the motorcycle club members normally parked their bikes. *In for a penny*, he thought. "Since we're headed to the same place"—*please God*—"can I hitch a ride? My car's in the shop." He'd been planning on bussing it, but this would at least give the guy a solid excuse to make it all the way to Andy's house, and with the car's brakes being worked on, it wasn't a lie.

"You wanna ride with me?" Something of wonder rumbled through the sweet-sounding baritone voice, accompanied by what sounded very much like a dark thread of desire. "I never…" His breath sounded shaky, and Andy pressed harder against his hand, willing the man to feel how his heart beat faster at the idea, too. *You're not alone, promise.* "Sure. I can do that. Okay." The biker nodded, seeming to convince himself. "Okay." That repeat of the word was stronger, filled with conviction, and Andy pulled in a breath, encouraging the man with his gaze. *Keep going.* "You ever ride a bike?" Andy shook his head. "Okay." Andy got a quick lesson in what to do and more importantly, what not to, and then they were off.

Once on the road, Andy grinned as the air rushed past his ears, filling his head with white noise. He held tightly to the man's waistband on either side, keeping a few inches of space between their bodies. The biker had seemed to tense when Andy snugged up close at first, but relaxed as soon as he'd slipped farther back on the seat.

The turn to his house was coming up, so Andy leaned forwards and put his mouth near the guy's ear, half shouting, "Next right." The man nodded and turned his head slightly, and his mouth was right there, so close Andy couldn't help himself, angling his head to graze the corner of the biker's lips with a kiss. The man's eyes widened, and then he turned to face ahead, the bike leaning as they rounded the corner. He shifted slightly after they had straightened after the turn, and heat brushed Andy's chest from the guy's leather vest as the biker sagged backwards into him.

He took that as an invitation and shifted forwards, tucking his chin over the guy's shoulder, grinning at both the thrill of the solid form between his legs and the adventure of speeding down the street with nothing between him and disaster, except this man and his clearly evident skill with the machine. Filled with sudden confidence, Andy let one hand slip down the man's hip and curve around, fingertips grazing the front of his jeans. He sucked in a breath, surprised when he found a hard cock just waiting for his caress. The engine of the bike stuttered when he palmed the erection, evening back out when he kept a steady pressure instead of the teasing touch he'd begun with.

"Next left," he said, lips once again against the curve of the man's ear as he shifted his hand back up.

With the swiftly moving bike under him and the warm and solid presence of the man in front of him, Andy felt intoxicated by the moment, poised on the cusp of anything and everything.

Mister man
Myron

"Where are you going, mister man?" Light and sweet, the lilting voice of a child came from behind him, and Myron turned with a jerk, surprised into dropping one of his boots. It hit the hallway floor with a thud, bouncing off the leg of the entryway table and tumbling to come to rest at the feet of the cutest little girl Myron had ever seen.

"I have to go to work." A harmless excuse, and one even a child would likely accept at face value. She'd wave him away, and he'd walk out the door, safely escaped with no one the wiser.

"Papa says I can't get up until a grownup is awake." Her lips pulled to the side as she chewed on a thought. "You're awake." She tipped her head towards a shoulder, the motion endearing. Her features were all seriousness when she said, "Grownups make breakfast in the morning. Can you help me? Can you make pancakes? I want pancakes."

Myron shook his head, and her bottom lip had started trembling before he even got the refusal out. "I can't, sweetness. I have to go."

Lip still quivering, she stared at him.

He stared at her. *Shhhh*, he thought. *I just wanna get out of here.*

When her nose scrunched up—which was adorable, but also telegraphed an audible version of the unsteady lip—he winked and then stuck out his tongue. It was instinctive and silly, something he remembered doing with his baby sister back when times were better, but it had the desired response. She giggled, and Myron was lost. He could no more deny this tiny princess her demand for pancakes than he could stop the world from turning, and he suddenly realized he didn't want to.

"Pancakes it is."

This little princess was named Natalya. He knew because the plaque on her door announced it. On the way to the kitchen, he glanced inside and saw an explosion of pinks and purples, décor clearly organized by a little girl who had a love of unicorns and hippos, mostly clad in tutus, because that was reflected in her plushie collection. *Adorable.* Myron smiled as he followed Natalya to the kitchen. That expression died as he thought about the discovery of a master bedroom last night, all the way down at the end of the hall.

Andy had told him to make himself at home. That had been right before the man had fallen asleep, worn out and boneless from an orgasm he'd drunkenly declared "the best I've ever had." Myron had taken him at his word and explored the house a little after he'd cleaned up, finding things he knew his brain would puzzle over for weeks to come.

That bedroom was huge, decorated with a tasteful mix of grays and browns. The headboard of dark wood paired with dressers, plural, were offset with more muted accents tucked in amidst artwork and bedding. Plush bedding on a huge king-size bed in a room that looked entirely unused. He'd studied the space for a long time, turning over all reasons he could think of why Andy would choose to sleep in what was clearly a guest room.

Maybe he just takes his hookups there. Myron's nose wrinkled like Natalya's at the thought, not liking how that felt.

He'd curtailed his explorations there with a headful of questions, showering quickly before returning to the double bed in Andy's room. It had been a rare moment of selfishness, but instead of leaving like he should have, Myron had granted himself permission to slide back between the sheets, tucked close along Andy's back and wrapped his arms around the sturdy body in front of him. He'd echoed Andy's contented, sleepy sigh, dropped a kiss on the back of his neck, and burrowed his nose underneath curly hair as he breathed in deeply.

When he'd woken, it was disoriented and wary, because sleepovers were not something Myron did. Hell, none of this, not a bit of it jibed with his normal routine. He didn't date, didn't hook up, didn't dare aim at so lofty a goal as a boyfriend. He had the club, and Mason, and his goal was making sure he lived up to the trust the man had put in him so long ago.

As he and Natalya—who preened every time he said her name—worked to mix up a batch of pancakes, Myron kept most of his attention on her, but his mind often drifted back over the previous night.

After the call came in, he'd gotten to the bar in record time to find Brute's girl, Bexley, already settled at the bar, but thankfully embedded in a group of regulars. She'd been roofied here once, which explained why Brute was so wary. The guy had been someone traveling through, and once the incident was brought to the attention of the bar's employees and regulars, they'd joined forces with the Rebels in keeping Bex safe. Knowing there were always eyes looking out for her didn't change their brother's concern, so any Rebel available to take the call was more than willing. Family first.

Myron had tucked into a corner, settled himself at a table and waited. Behind the bar had been empty, which wasn't unusual if the bartender was working alone. On his previous trip, he'd seen her disappearing into the backroom to quickly change out kegs or find a replacement bottle of booze, so Myron expected his wait for an unwanted beer wouldn't be long. He'd been distracted by his phone, responding to a series of text questions from a member when he'd heard someone clear their throat nearby.

Myron had looked up into the clearest, bluest eyes he'd ever seen. An ice-blue that should have looked cold, but didn't, the tanned skin surrounding them lending warmth. Circled by ridiculously long lashes those eyes stared back at him, and Myron felt heat curl in his chest, climbing his neck to his cheeks.

"What'll you have?" The lyrical, deep voice had seemed to come from a far distance away, wrapping around him like flannel sheets, dragging at his skin in a way that made every nerve ending come alive. He ignored the question, focused instead on those damned eyes, watching as they darkened. "You see something you like, honey?" That same voice, but it had developed a distinct flirty tone, and recognition had jolted Myron out of the daze those damned eyes had put him in.

"What?" God, he'd hated how he sounded. His voice had been soft and startled, and so at odds with the persona he had to present to the world all the time, he had hardly recognized it.

"To drink. Do you know what you want?" Myron's gaze had dropped to the man's lips, watching them move and stretch as he smiled, seeing the dance of a clever tongue behind lips and teeth. In that moment he'd known all this man would have to do was ask and Myron would do anything...anything at all, just to have those eyes and that smile directed his way again.

That need had slipped past his guard, opening up wounds he didn't know he still carried. Standing in Mouse's kitchen, Myron flinched at the painful memory. *Andy*, he thought, remembering the request as they'd fumbled off their clothes last night. *"Mouse is the guy who works the bar. Here, I'm just Andy."*

"Mister man, what's your name?" Here was a question he could answer finally, having dodged all her others about why he was there, and why Papa was such a sleepyhead.

"Myron, sweetness. My name is Myron."

"Myron is Papa's good friend, baby girl. I hope you haven't been too big a pest." Myron and Natalya both jerked around to look at the doorway. Myron let his gaze take in Andy's casual, rumpled at-home Sunday-morning look, hair a mess and lips still swollen from their kisses last night. "Morning." That rumbled greeting paired with a salacious wink had Myron's dick perking up, pulsing with a renewed desire that sent a thrill through him. A strange look swept across Andy's features for a moment and then he seemed to shake it off, strolling towards where Myron stood next to Natalya. "You look good in my kitchen." He got close and reached out to place a hand on Myron's waist, giving a squeeze as he bent to press a kiss to Natalya's head. "What's for breakfast, little Talya?"

Andy straightened and was so close Myron felt heat from his body all along his front. Andy gave him another squeeze that sizzled along Myron's nerves. Then, as if he knew his effect on Myron, one corner of his mouth lifted in a smirk as he stepped to the side, leaving Myron weaving drunkenly in his wake. That's what had happened last night, too; Myron had gotten drunk. Not on booze, he'd only had one beer at the bar, but on the heady knowledge that a man like Andy had sensed his attraction and then acted on it, making it clear that he liked Myron's attention, and more—returned it.

"Pancakes!" Talya crowed, throwing her arms in the air as if having pancakes for breakfast were a lifelong dream finally being realized.

"Then let's get busy." As easily as that Andy had accepted Myron's invasion of his home, working alongside him until they finished preparing the simple meal and followed Talya into the dining room, plate of pancakes in hand.

That was the moment things began to go bad.

Just a stranger
Andy

Andy woke in a bed that had always seemed just slightly too small for two broad-shouldered men to sleep easily, unless they were cuddlers. Which he'd never been, not even in the first exhilarating rush of a new relationship. Certainly not with a casual hookup, or even one of the rare repeats he'd had over the years. But, something he'd discovered about himself last night was he *could* be—with the right man. He'd drifted up from his doze a couple of times to find himself wrapped around the biker in his bed like he was Andy's own personal snuggle bunny. The temperature in the house had been a little too warm—thermostat set for solo sleeping—and instead of moving apart, they'd quickly abandoned the blanket, keeping just the thin sheet. A move that proved to be chilly now that he was alone in the bed.

Alone.

His eyes opened a slit to see light creeping in around the blinds.

Well, hell.

Still hoping, he reached out, his palm encountering only cool, entirely rumpled sheets. *Fuck.*

It shouldn't have been a surprise that the apparently closeted biker abandoned his bed during the night. Andy had met enough of the Rebel Wayfarers members that when he'd caught what looked like curiosity in the man's eyes, he'd assumed his radar had gone wonky at first.

He remembered the first night the woman Bexley had come in. She was the sole reason the sleepy neighborhood bar had acquired new clientele. The sudden appearance of a massive, badly-scarred-but-still-badass-looking biker had been startling as he'd swept her up and out of the bar. It had been only minutes later that Andy had gotten the full story from the kitchen staff, which meant he hadn't put up any kind of fuss when two more burly bikers showed to drag the scumbag who had tried to drug her out the back door of the bar. A few days later she'd showed again, looking none the worse for wear, and her biker he-man had not only asked Andy to watch out for her, but clearly made the same request of his friends. These days it was like clockwork: if Bexley showed, he was guaranteed at least one biker coming in as well, their focus always on her.

Until last night.

Late summer, a lot of the locals were away at lake houses or on vacation, which meant his night had started slow. Stools and seats had gradually filled with regulars, including Bexley, which Andy had known meant the appearance of one of her leather-clad cavalry was imminent. He stuck to what he did best, joking and serving drinks, and tried unsuccessfully to shake off the slow night blues. Then, oh then, he caught his first sight of a brand-new, shiny biker dude at a two-top in the corner.

The biker must have slipped in when he wasn't looking and by the time Andy saw him had focused on his phone, firm chin tilted down, tousled hair angled across his face. Even without looking up he made an impression. A very good one. So, the first time Andy waited on a nearby table he'd paused, stepped close and asked if the guy needed anything. *Tell me you want me, baby.* It had been a no-go with that wish, but there remained *something* that drew Andy in.

Everything about the wiry man was memorable. Not just how appealing he looked in his vest or jeans, although those pants had looked like they fit *very* well. Every time Andy had turned from ringing up a new sale on the register to sweep the crowd with his gaze, checking levels of bottles and glasses, the biker at the tiny table in the back had been staring at him. Not glaring, although Andy was accustomed to some of that, men who seemed personally offended that he wasn't shy about batting for the other team. No, Andy had become convinced the luscious and lickable biker had been staring at him with interest. There was just...a presence about him.

Myron, the patch on his vest had read, and the name fit who he seemed to be. Slightly stuffy, but definitely a name that begged to be whispered during a kiss.

Lying alone in bed Andy murmured it again, feeling his lips pursing with the sounds. "Myron."

He pressed the heels of his hands to his forehead before rolling to the edge of the bed. Sitting there, he could hear tiny noises that signaled movement in the house. Andy shook his head. Talya was normally so good about staying in her room until he'd gotten up. Glancing at his phone, he saw it was early yet and sighed as he pushed up from the bed. Myron clearly hadn't hung around long, and Andy's eyes felt full of gravel on only three hours of sleep.

The closer he got to the kitchen, however, the less certain he was that Myron had actually made it out of the house. Sure enough, when he peeked around the corner, there stood the tough-looking biker, hair adorably mussed, with powdered sugar smeared along the edge of his stubble-rough jaw. Natalya was poised on her stepstool next to him, hands steadying the bowl as Myron dipped a cup of batter to pour in a careful circle on the griddle.

"Good job, mister man." Talya's praise made Myron's lips quirk in a lopsided grin, and Andy stepped out, losing Talya's next question in his rush to make sure this was real. This gorgeous man truly was standing in his kitchen after he'd expected to never have this again, calling his little girl "sweetness" simply because she was.

The next few minutes were exciting and mundane in the same breath. There were no awkward morning-after jitters in his belly, and Andy let himself lean close, capturing Myron's lips in a chaste kiss in a moment while Talya was otherwise occupied. He kept her busy with setting the table and then organized their trek to the dining room. It was almost surreal, the happiness it gave him to watch Myron move through his house, the biker doing it with a level of comfort Andy found addicting.

He tried to stay in the moment, not wanting to read too much into the whole encounter. Still...it was hard because he wanted this, craved more of the quietly shy man he had met last night, and desired at least one more taste of the sweet lover he'd discovered lay under the denim and leather.

He wanted...more.

***

Myron

Andy smiled as he pulled out the seat at the head of the table while Talya moved towards what looked to be her usual chair, booster seat strapped tightly in place. Myron reached for the chair to Andy's right. This would place their little group of three clustered around one end of the table, allowing for easy conversation. Something Myron found himself very much looking forward to.

Then tiny Talya looked up at him, wide eyes swimming with tears as her face fell, pain and sadness suffusing her features. "That's Daddy's chair." Myron froze and looked to Andy who was staring at Talya, a matching mask of pain stretching across his face, distorting the smile he'd worn all morning and turning it to a twisted grimace.

Myron glanced around the room, seeing pictures he'd ignored earlier, candid photos of a smiling Andy standing next to a handsome man in a suit who was tall and lean, a strong arm wrapped possessively around Andy. A younger Talya was balanced on one of Andy's hips, her hands on the other man's face, pulling him around to face the camera. *Daddy.* Andy had a man, that's why they'd fucked in the guest bedroom and not the master. *Can't have the sheets smelling like a stranger when Daddy got home.*

Andy hadn't argued when Myron found an immediate and pressing need to leave, following him to the door with downcast eyes. A whispered, "I'm sorry," the only thing said between them. The, *I can't do this* remained unspoken. Nothing else needed to be said. Myron was sorry too.

I wish

Myron, one week later

"Jesus." He panted for breath as he reached to where his phone was propped against the wall. On the other end of the line, Andy did the same thing, the angle of the video changing from the artful presentation of a no-longer-erect cock to his sweating, smiling face. "You're killing me."

"If you'd jack *with* me instead of after, you'd end these calls in a better mood." Andy laughed, light and carefree. He was still out of breath, his chest rising and falling fast but his relaxed smile was slow as molasses, making Myron's heart lurch. "Did you like that one? You requested more dirty talk, did I deliver?"

Myron reached down and palmed his cock, touch too familiar to be erotic. When they were like this, he would sometimes get far enough into the scene he could convince his body that it was Andy's hand. *Not tonight.* He hissed in frustration.

The reason for that filtered under the doorway, sounds of the party downstairs making their way to his room on the second floor of the Chicago clubhouse. Myron adjusted the earbud he had in place, ensuring there'd be no eavesdroppers on this very private conversation. He kept his voice quiet, pitching it just loud enough Andy could hear him through the mic. "I did like it. It was perfect." Having his own private porn streaming on demand was more than a novelty, it had become the highlight of his days. "So perfect."

Myron hadn't lost the bartender's number. He hadn't lost the memories of what they'd done, either. He'd managed to wait a whole day before texting the first time, covering his eagerness to talk to Andy by asking about a zoo expedition Talya had rattled on about as they made pancakes. They'd quickly fallen into a routine of texts and calls on days Andy was off.

It didn't seem to matter to his dick that Andy had a regular man in his life. At the beginning of every call, Myron promised himself he'd bring up the man in the picture, but then he'd imagine watching Andy close off, expression shuttering, and he couldn't do it. As long as they kept it to this, kept the distance between them while maintaining intimacy, Myron could tell himself it didn't matter. The only thing that mattered was Andy's smile, his excitement, and yes, his dirty talk didn't hurt, either. Myron knew if he asked and Andy answered, the walls that kept them safe would fall, and the world would rush back in.

Myron's position in the Rebel organization meant unless things were going down, he could carve out an hour or two nearly anytime. Without letting himself ponder what it might mean, he'd tried to make a point of doing so each time Andy texted. This connection between them—whatever it was—had stayed strong, so much stronger than he could have predicted. For all he liked his spreadsheets and formulas, and the probability of being able to plot out any given path, he'd found himself happily winging it with Andy.

"Are you coming back here soon? I didn't hate this house as much when you were in it." Andy's pupils were still blown, dark and earnest, kissable pink lips puffy from biting them as he'd jacked and fingered himself. Words unguarded, undoubtedly by the orgasm, he murmured, "I liked you here. Made everything...better." He shifted backwards on the bed and grabbed his boxers, discarded early on during the call, and used them to halfheartedly wipe down before collapsing again. Andy's face was nearer the phone when he whispered, "I want to see you again, Myron. Want to hold you."

"I don't know. I've told you things are a little...unsettled here." That was an understatement. Diamante MC was stirring the pot again, and Mason had called an all-officers meeting earlier tonight, pulling in men from a half a dozen chapters. That was the reason for the big blowout happening downstairs. Myron knew if he walked down the steps to the main floor, he'd be presented with a dozen different varieties of what Andy had just shown him, all female versions. "I'm gonna go now." Andy's bottom lip stuck out on cue, showing without words how he felt about Myron ending the call before he finished on his end. Voice he could accommodate, and had, his whispered pleas hit the air alongside Andy's deeper commands. Video was trickier, harder to refute if someone captured any of the footage. "Brat. You gave me a lot to use for inspiration."

"At least there's that." Andy grinned, but it died fast, falling away. "I wish you were here."

"Me, too." It wasn't a lie. He wanted a world where that was possible. Where he could be the main attraction in Andy's life. Heavy footfalls came down the hallway towards his room, the only door at this end of the building, which meant they were coming for him. He leaned towards the phone as he shoved his cock into his pants, wincing when his not-quite-wilted erection snagged on a button. "I gotta go. Text me."

"You know I will." Andy pursed his lips, and Myron disconnected with a smile, arching up to settle his pants around his hips.

"Myron." *Thud. Thud. Thud.* "Sorry to wake you, brother. Boss wants a word."

"Be right there." He listened to the receding footsteps, slowing his breathing. He'd never before begrudged the Rebels anything. They'd saved him. No part of his life was his own, and that was how it just was.

How it needed to be. No matter if it wasn't how Mason saw it, Myron was body and soul a Rebel.

Sometimes, though.

I wish...

He didn't finish the thought. Angling off the bed and stamping into his boots, he then reached for the doorknob.

What I need

Myron, one week later

Standing just outside the back door of the Rebel Wayfarers Fort Wayne clubhouse, Myron surveyed the clumps of people standing here and there. Whenever there was a mixed-club party, there was always a certain amount of tension. Inviting others into the RWMC house, even friendly groups like this club from Florida, Myron and the other officers were on guard for any missteps.

Not that he expected anything to go sideways. No, he was so confident it would be without incident, he was even counting down until he could reasonably leave. The Jailbreakers MC had proven themselves over the past months, eagerly meeting any Rebel demands, and more than once coming back with greater than expected results. Sparks, their president, had worked to ingratiate himself with Mason in a way which cemented the relations between the clubs. This party was supposed to be the celebration of Sparks and Mason coming to an agreement, and the result of that pact meant every Jailbreakers member present sported a shiny new support patch for the RWMC.

Myron bent over and fished in an open cooler, coming up with a dripping bottle. He grinned, remembering the look on Sparks' face as the Rebel prospects lugged in the beer this afternoon. If there were any inklings of trouble, the Rebels would have been only serving kegs or cans, and Sparks had known it. The expression on his face said he'd very much appreciated the implicit vote of confidence. *Sometimes it's the little things.* Myron sighed as he twisted the cap off, tossing it into a nearby box of trash. *Pretty full*, he thought and tipped his head to catch the eye of a prospect. Wordlessly, he pointed and got a chin lift in response.

"Brother," he heard, that single word all the warning he got before a hand clapped on his shoulder, gripped hard and shoved him to the side before rocking him back. Twisting around, he ducked out from under the clasp and shook his head, looking up at Gunny. "We gotta get you a gal, Myron. Get Slate's GeeMa lookin' at the church socials again. Some of those e-mails were a fuckin' riot."

Jesus, not this again. He didn't let his dismay show, just kept a smile steady on his face as he demurred, the twin tactics of distraction and deflection second nature. "Yeah, a riot. Gunny...brother, I do all right. In fact, I feel the need to head back to Chicago soon." The implication was he had a special piece of ass there, and when

Gunny's face lit with a grin, even though it had been his intent, he nearly groaned in response.

"Myron, you dog. Why didn't you say so?" Gunny looked around, seeming to search for something and then Myron's blood ran cold when he heard him say, "Bones, your brother-in-law's got him a piece of tail, and you didn't say anything?"

Bones was involved with Myron's sister, Ester, a relationship that was as complicated as the day was long. He was based in Chicago along with Myron, and hadn't been expected to attend this party. Myron turned and saw Bones sauntering their direction, gaze on a never-ending loop around the yard, always on guard for trouble.

"Myron. It is good to see you again. My Ester misses her Ronnie." Bones flashed a smile, teeth bright against his mix of dusky skin and tattoos. "When will you return to our Chicago?"

"I'll head back after the weekend." He stretched and took a final drink from the beer, tossing it to the now-emptied box. "Wanted to make sure the Jailbreakers party happened like Mason wanted."

"And it did. Well done." Bones sketched a teasing bow. "I will be going back tonight. My Ester still has nerves when I am too long gone. Anyone I should speak to on your behalf when I return?"

Not in Chicago. Mouth clamped tight as he shook his head, Myron was filled with terror at the idea of Bones speaking to the one person who had so effortlessly occupied his mind the past few weeks.

No, he wouldn't be asking any of his brothers to carry messages to this particular crush anytime soon. *I'll deliver my own, thank you very much.*

Memories drew a picture in his mind of button-down shirt tucked into too-tight jeans, guyliner making already startling eyes breathtaking, and sparkling earrings adorning skin that begged for teeth marks. *I want to see him.* A smile that went on for days, with a plump bottom lip that could bow into the sweetest arc. *I want to touch him.*

Myron widened his stance, making a little more room for his thickening cock. *I could be at the bar in fifteen minutes.* With a single text, he knew Andy would be waiting for him in the backroom of the bar. *Can I do this?* Myron glanced around the party again and lifted his chin. "I got somewhere to be." He deliberately phrased it that way, knowing they'd take that as a sidelong mention of club business. *Camouflage.* "See you back in Chicago." His muscles jumped with nervous tension, because Bones could just as easily offer to come with, and given his position in the club, Myron wouldn't be able to turn him down. He relaxed when the men offered only a warrior's shake, fists pounding against his back in goodbye. *They trust me.* This wasn't a betrayal of that trust; it was just him taking what he needed.

Sideways

Andy, two weeks later

He leaned against the kitchen cabinet and rubbed the back of his neck with one hand. It had been a hell of a long week. Ever since he'd brought Talya home from the hospital seven days ago, his gut had been churning with a near constant panic. It had buried him, sweeping over him like a wave of bitter fear right after he'd walked out of the building full of professionals, his arms full of precious little girl.

Andy understood in his head that a tonsillectomy was a common, normal childhood surgery. Easy peasy, a few days of minor pain handled via judicious application of the frozen goodness of popsicles. If having her tonsils and adenoids removed would keep her from having the near constant sore throat and resulting infections they'd been battling, it was an easy decision. Back in the doctor's office, when Andy had been looking around at the man's impressive array of framed certificates covering the walls, the process seemed logical.

His head might know, but his gut was a different story. Post-surgery, it was killing him to see his little girl feeling sore and grumpy, her normally bright voice dampened to a painful rasp as she recovered. *My little girl.* Sometimes even thinking those words felt surreal.

Talya wasn't his biological child, but he loved her fiercely, nonetheless. She was his, dammit, his and Roger's. He and Talya had already been through so much. It didn't seem fair she had to deal with this, too.

Andy and his partner, Roger Danfort, had created a close family unit with the three of them for the few years the two men had been together. He and Roger had met at the bar where Andy worked, and six months of stilted conversation later had a fumbling first date. That was followed by another, and another, until it seemed like they'd always been a couple. Even if the sex hadn't been explosive, they were compatible, liking the same kinds of things. Once Andy had met the then tiny Talya, he'd known he needed to be part of raising the amazing little girl. He'd quickly moved in with Roger and expected to live happily ever after.

He sighed. *Not in the cards.*

Roger had been working overseas, a two-week contract in London. For ten days he'd sent countless pictures home for Andy to share with Talya. He had called and video chatted every spare moment. Then...nothing, a three-day silence that had terrified Andy. It had been a coworker of Roger's who finally called and broke the news. There'd been a terrible accident, and Roger was dead, killed when his rental was broadsided by a truck. Andy wasn't listed on his emergency contacts, and while his employer knew Roger had a child, the only number on file had been an old one for his mother, long since disconnected.

Roger had been a late-in-life child, and Mother Danfort was a widow in her late seventies when he died. While she might have been remote emotionally, she wasn't a bigot, and from Roger's stories, had supported Roger when he came out as a young adult.

Andy closed his eyes tightly, forcing back the burn at the unwelcome memories.

That had been almost two years ago. Roger's death had signaled a time in his life Andy didn't like to dwell on, because it had been so hard. Grief and terror equal companions for months. In many ways, it seemed he'd never moved past it all.

Roger had adopted Talya before he and Andy had become a couple. Since the state they lived in didn't recognize same-sex marriage, even if they'd had a commitment ceremony, adding Andy to her birth certificate as one of two fathers hadn't been an option. All of which meant Roger's death had left Natalya without a guardian in the eyes of the law. Just getting Roger's body back for a funeral had been hard enough, but fighting at the same time to keep Talya sleeping in her own bed had made for a nightmarish few weeks.

While Mother Danfort helped where she could, if it hadn't been for Andy's grandmother, he didn't know what he would've done. Ever his staunch supporter, she had helped navigate the exhausting legal hurdles so Talya could stay with him.

My little girl. Andy had become the most important person in her life. And she was the most important one in his.

Now, one week post-surgery, what seemed like the worst of it behind them, she was resting in the living room. Piled on the couch with her favorite stuffed animal in her arms, she was watching cartoons that were blaring from the TV. Talya also had a wide assortment of juices and pudding cups on a nearby tray. She seemed to be picky today, deeming every offering, "Yucky tasting." The coughs wracking her tiny body were the worst, though. In fact, even now Andy could still hear her coughing over the noise. He cocked his head to listen closely, alarmed at how painful each cough sounded.

She'd been doing that a lot over the last couple of days, a part of the healing process the doctor had warned about. *It's normal*, he reminded himself. Everything was normal. Still listening to her, he reached into the cabinet and pulled out a coffee mug, placing it on the counter next to the single-serve machine, knowing he would need a pick-me-up before the evening was over.

He tilted his head, again listening attentively, and now heard the unmistakable gagging sound of a six-year-old little girl about to vomit. "Oh, no," he muttered, grabbed a dishtowel and turned to the door just in time to see Talya stumble into view. She looked at him, her dark hair tumbled around her tiny face as she bent double, most of her recent meal of soup forcefully ejecting and making a puddle on the floor. "Papa," she cried, arm wrapped around her belly, one hand lifting to her face. "It hurts." She was pale, paler than he remembered, and he immediately decided a trip to urgent care was in their future as he strode quickly towards her.

That was when his world went sideways. Before he could reach her, Talya coughed again and again, her small form shuddering with each uncontrollable movement. She cupped both hands under her mouth and looked at him, eyes round with pain and fear. Talya lifted them to show him what she'd seen. They were filled with red.

Hold it together
Andy

"Do something," Andy yelled at the nurse standing beside the reception desk at the ER. Talya stirred in his arms, no doubt reacting to the sheer volume of his voice. He and Roger had always joked about who would have to be the bad cop when she got older, because both men were normally quietly spoken. Right now, however, the last thing he cared about was minding his manners. He was terrified. "She's bleeding so much!" She was, too. The entire front of her nightgown was coated in a broad swath of red, freshened every time Talya vomited again. That had been the most terrifying moment in the car, when she'd thrown up a second time, the bowl she held falling away as her throat convulsed painfully and he'd realized that more blood had to be pouring down the back of her throat than had leaked from her nose and mouth. "She just had her tonsils taken out."

The nurse finally jarred into motion. It felt as though it had taken hours for her to catch up, but when she did, it was with lightning fast reactions. She slapped a button on the desk and started yelling code words, initiating a milling buzz of activity in moments. A man in scrubs gently examined Talya in Andy's arms, ignoring the hiccupping cries to "stay with Papa" that tore at Andy's heart. An Australian accent did nothing to soften the urgency of his instructions, "She needs to be upstairs, STAT."

Andy stared at him, murmuring to Talya, "It'll be okay honey. Papa's right here. You're gonna be all right." *Please God, let me be right.*

A male nurse directed them up the hallway and to an elevator behind secure doors, moving at a fast clip as he swiped open the doors, Andy hot on his heels. He heard the overhead speakers paging her doctor's name, followed by another code. Andy crammed into the elevator, watching Talya's face. She seemed to grow paler by the second, and he felt his heart stop in his chest as her tiny head toppled sideways, landing against his shoulder with a thud Andy felt down to his soul. "What's happening?" *Please God, make her be okay.*

"She's lost a lot of blood." The nurse stated the obvious, and through his fear, Andy recognized a return of the fury that'd had him howling down in reception. The man seemed to sense the change in the atmosphere in the tiny space they shared because he angled a glance over his shoulder, pinning Andy with a look. "We're going to take good care of your little girl, Mr. Kasmouski. As if she were our own. We'll do everything she needs. You need to hold it together." The elevator dinged, and just as the doors opened, he spoke firmly, offering sage advice that told Andy just how desperate Talya's condition might be, comforting words aside. "If you have a partner or good friend, call them. Get yourself some support and get yourself into a place in your head where you can be the best you can be for this little girl." The door opened and the nurse strode out, put his back to a set of doors as he yelled, "Open the suite." He lifted his arms in a silent demand and Andy placed his daughter—his heart—into the man's hands. The doors swung open behind him, and Andy stared at Talya, her beautiful face hidden behind her hair as the nurse moved through, turned, and was gone.

Another nurse was there, hand on Andy's arm, gently directing him towards an open door to the side. Once in the surgical waiting room, with her promises of providing regular updates still ringing in his ears, Andy did as the male nurse suggested and placed a call. It went straight to voice mail and when he looked at the chat icon saw it was on Do Not Disturb. Andy chewed his lip for another moment then pulled out a card Brute had given him, a single number listed underneath the skull logo he'd seen on the back of so many leather vests and jackets.

"CH, whatcha need?" The rough voice answering the phone wasn't one he recognized, and Andy stumbled a moment, searching for words. "Yo, ain't got all day. Got a need? Spit 'er out."

Voice shaking so he scarcely recognized it himself, Andy asked, "Myron. Is Myron available?"

Party line
Myron

"Myron, grab the phone, brother."

Pulled from his review of the most recent forecast for the Rebel Fort Wayne businesses, Myron stared at Goose, his mired-in-numbers brain taking a moment to catch up. The clubhouse had an old-fashioned phone attached to the wall behind the main room's bar, and Goose was standing, arm extended, handset dangling from his fingers. His friend and patch brother grinned broadly and swung the device back and forth, like a hypnotist's coin dangling from a string. "Earth to Myron. Come in, Myron."

"Houston, we have a problem," he muttered and pushed away from the table. He dropped the printout on top of the piles of paper already littering the surface and stood. "Coming." Reaching for the phone, he rolled his eyes when Goose first jerked it away, then laughed and handed it over. He put it to his ear and announced himself. "Myron."

Dead air.

He glared at Goose as he realized he hadn't even heard the damn phone ring. *Damn jokester.* Now he'd have to get his head back around wherever he'd been in the spreadsheet—a sound came through the phone interrupting his thoughts, sounding like a generic announcement intercom. Myron listened intently and made out the steady sound of someone breathing, in and out. "Hello? This is Myron."

He stood straight, eyes wide when he heard, "I didn't know who to call." Even upset, that voice was distinctive, flat Midwest drawl and all. There was no mistaking the bartender he couldn't get enough of.

"Mouse?" Across the room he saw Brute's head come up, scarred mien swinging to face him. *This is all Brute's fault, anyway.* Brute well knew who Mouse was, even if he didn't know what had happened the first time Myron saw him while playing babysitter to Bexley.

He and Andy had only been seeing each other for a few weeks, and so far, Myron had been careful to steer things away from what could be a disaster if something like this happened. "Is everything okay?" Myron turned his back to the room, pulling the phone close in an attempt to create a pocket of privacy for himself, but there was a reason the phone was placed where it was, and still attached to the wall like a junior high school boy's nightmare. The only thing that would give less privacy was if it were a party line, something Myron only vaguely remembered from the time before his parents died.

"I'm at the hospital." Andy's voice broke, going high as he croaked out, "Talya's...Myron, something happened to Natalya."

"Where are you?" Myron was already running through logistics in his head. They hadn't chatted this week. Between Myron dancing attendance on club meetings and Andy's reports that Talya wasn't feeling well, texting had been all they'd managed. But there was no question in his mind he'd be going to the hospital, because if Andy needed him, he would damn well be there. If Talya needed him— *Please, God, let her be okay.* He'd ridden his bike down from Chicago, but he'd rather not park it in a public lot on his own. If there were several bikes together, no worries, but a single bike was easy to steal. All it took was three men and a trailer, and his iron would be lost. The club had both a van and truck assigned to this chapter, so he'd have a ride anyway.

Andy gave him the information for the hospital, and told him where the surgical waiting room was located. *Surgery. Shit.* That gave Myron pause, because surgery on such a little girl was frightening to consider. *How did her not feeling well jump to needing surgery?* Talya was only six, small for her age, and the thought of her going under the knife had to be eating at Andy.

"Can you come? It's just me...and..." Andy pulled in a shaking breath. "Can you come?" *How is he there alone? Where is Talya's daddy?*

"Andy?" He waited until he heard an affirming sound. "I'll be there soon. Hang in there, man." He made a promise he knew he couldn't back up, but was helpless to offer any other comfort. "She's going to be okay." Blowing out a breath on a steady exhale, he hung up the phone and tried to compose his expression before turning around. He was glad he'd taken those few seconds when he realized every man in the room was focused on him. He wasn't the only RWMC member who'd taken a turn watching over Bex at the bar, which meant he wasn't the only one who knew Mouse. "His little girl's in surgery." That would explain to the group what was going on, but not why Mouse had reached out to *him*, out of all the people he could call.

Family came first in the RWMC, something their founder and president had hammered home time and again. Mason had a way with words and wasn't shy about using them to get what he wanted. Like every great leader, he seemed to have an innate understanding about what it took to wrangle the best out of every man under his patch. For many, it was knowing their family would be taken care of, no matter what.

As far as his brothers knew, Myron had done just the same as them. Gone to the bar, nursed a beer or two while staying focused on Bexley. Their very presence in the bar providing an extension of their brother, keeping his woman safe when Brute couldn't.

And sure, that's what Myron had done the first time he'd gotten the call to babysit Bexley. *Andy wasn't working that night*, he reminded himself. No, his introduction to the out-and-proud Andy hadn't come until a few weeks later, and Myron remembered the feeling in his gut when he'd waltzed into the bar expecting to see the tall brunette working only to find the handsome Andy instead. That had been a memorable night, Myron's first real encounter with a man who didn't hide his sexuality. *And it was Andy.*

Myron had been closeted for...ever, it seemed like. After figuring out what he liked from a relatively young age, he'd never known a day when he wasn't on guard with his actions or words. Even during his time spent in the homeless shelters around Chicago, any quick, desperate encounters that seemed to last only moments in duration had all happened in darkened nooks and crannies. Desire or need hidden behind bravado in public, prowess with fighting best on display instead of what so many would see as a weakness.

Then had come the truly desperate days, where those furtive actions took on a coating of shame, the sparse clink of coins flicked at his feet on the worst days, or crumpled, filthy bills tucked into a back pocket on only slightly better ones. Body spent and mind weary, Myron had been lost within the unwashed ranks of the forgotten for so long, he had begun to feel invisible, seated at a long table with so many other homeless men, trying to be unobtrusive as he tucked spare slices of bread into his often-mended pockets.

He'd been seated like that one night, one of the lucky few queued up early enough to secure not only a meal but a bed, mind occupied with a jar of buttons a volunteer had handed him on his way into the shelter. A voice, deep and amused, gently joking as if they'd been friends forever had asked him what he was doing. Myron could remember the exact words if pressed, but what had cemented itself deeply in his mind was the face of the man standing across the table, basket of bread in hand like any other volunteer. Older, but not too, only a decade or so in age difference—which now, years later, seemed a laughably small distance—but immeasurably older in experience.

That had been his first introduction to Davis Mason, the national president and founder of the Rebel Wayfarers MC.

Mason, the man who had saved him.

Myron blinked fast, unexpected sentimentality creeping up on him without warning. Mason would say that Myron had saved himself, by having the courage to reach out and take the hand offered, but Myron knew better. Before Mason and the RWMC, he'd been trapped performing an ever-shorter arc of attempted escapes from that life, all doomed to failure, and all with the same eventual destination. It was a minor miracle that he hadn't gotten tangled up in drugs or drink while running from the depressing destitution of his life, and his resolve had worn thin by that night. The man seated to his right on the shelter's bench had already offered him an out, promise of a sharp-needled amnesia if Myron would get on his knees after lights-out. *Never know if I'd have taken it.*

"Myron, brother. You're goin', right?" He jumped and looked around, seeing three men had approached him. Gunny was closest and held a hand out, palm down like someone would do with an agitated dog. Goose and Brute stood just behind him, their broad shoulders blocking Myron from view of the rest of the room. "You need someone to drive you to the hospital?"

Just like that, with the raw concern in Gunny's voice, he knew they'd read the situation...read him, and *knew.* Myron took a step back, a bump from his shoulders jarring the handset off the hook, cord tangling his arm as it fell. The ghost of a blow flickered across his skin, remembered sensation of hard-striking leather making his head swim. He shrugged away from that and slid to the side, muscles tensed and ready for what he expected would come next. It was no secret that the MC world was custom made for men. Men who liked to drink and party. Men who liked to fuck women and lots of them, being chased by fender bunnies in every town. Men who were all-in when it came to breaking any of society's rules. Any that is, except this one.

Myron shook his head and lifted his chin, glaring at the three men that for years, he'd counted as friends as well as brothers under the patch. "No," he bluffed, schooling his face to hide his sudden anger and grief. "I'm good, brother." The word slipped out, and he waited for one of them to throw it back into his face, waited for them to follow whatever unspoken code they felt necessary.

"I texted Bulldog." Brute's voice was quiet, rough as always, vocal cords forever damaged by the injuries taken during his last overseas deployment. He'd become friends with the ER doc who knew more about bikers than anyone would expect. Bulldog had somehow become a friend of the club just by being there during hard situations over the years, now an invited guest at their parties. If he were working and Mouse took his daughter to the ER, he might know the situation. Brute's features were unreadable as he delivered the next verbal blow. "He said to hurry."

Fuck.

"Myron." That was Brute, someone who knew Mouse well, and since Mouse wasn't one to hide away, he would surely know everything. "Let me drive you." When Myron would have argued, he shook his head. "You're not fit, brother. Goose can follow and bring me back. I'll leave the truck for you for later."

Bulldog said to hurry.

Myron nodded and turned to follow Brute out of the clubhouse, leaving everything he'd found worth living for behind. Maybe for the last time.

I need him

Andy

Andy slumped backwards into the uncomfortable hospital seat with a sickening sense of relief as he watched the hospital chaplain lead a sobbing woman out of the waiting room. When the chaplain had walked into the room accompanied by a surgeon, Andy's chest had seized, air clogging thick in his throat.

I just need to hold on. Myron will be here.

Since the single night Myron had spent in his bed, breakfast painfully truncated by an awkward wash of memories, there had been only a few quick encounters between the two men. Tiny slices of time where their lives glanced off each other. Like cue balls careening off the bumper of a pool table, they didn't stay in the same place long. When they were there, though—occupying the same space—it was extraordinary.

It wasn't without downfalls, however. Since officially coming out at eighteen, Andy had never tried to be with anyone deeply closeted, and he found being with Myron was equal parts frustrating and thrilling. His panicked alarm when Andy would initiate anything other than casual contact in public was only offset by an equally greedy hunger when they carved out a moment to be alone.

There'd been no more sleepovers, but after only having calls and video at first, over the past couple of weeks, they'd worked out a rhythm where at least once every few days Andy could be guaranteed a visitor at the end of his shift. He'd carry out the last load of trash to find Myron patiently waiting in the shadows.

The back room of the bar had ample vertical surfaces for Myron to push him against, and Andy eagerly went with the wordless demands, needing to get his hands on more of the broody man. The making out part of each meeting? *Beyond* good. He took his time, as if he were determined to explore every sensitive inch of flesh, and Myron was hands-down the best kisser Andy had ever been with. His kisses were an enlightening experience, every time, and Andy had come to anticipate those moments where they could be together, maybe more than he should. It was as if he came to life in Myron's hands, needing Myron's touch and caress to light up every nerve in his body. Shaking hands fumbling with shirts and belts, the strain and arch of their bodies as they sought out skin—just thinking about it always made Andy rock-hard in moments.

To fill the desire for each other in between visits, those phone and video calls were still regular. Frequent, and filled with filthy murmurs, they were too short to do anything except ratchet up a need that had become a constant companion for Andy. It was there, inside him, always bubbling just under the surface, ready to boil over the moment Myron was near.

Andy liked looking at him, too, especially when Myron didn't know he was. Just watching Myron interact with the other bikers in the bar filled him with pride. His man was held in high esteem. Even if no one knew Myron was his. That pride was balanced by an even greater sense of danger, because if Andy had been asked to think of a single group in the city who were not gay-friendly, it would be the biker gangs. Which meant Myron was walking a dangerous line by even as much as they'd managed.

I shouldn't have called. Andy ran his fingers through his hair, tugging hard enough to make him grimace. He might have unintentionally outed Myron to his friends, and that could be disastrous not only for them together, but for Myron. The club was his whole life; it showed in the way he talked about them, about the man Mason. *I shouldn't have.*

But I need him.

Perfect match

Myron

Riding shotgun in the truck, Myron scooted near the door, gripping the handle tightly.

Walking away from the clubhouse had been hard.

Myron shifted on the seat and felt Brute's gaze land on him like a blow. The man didn't go out much, not where people other than club could see him, but he hadn't hesitated to offer this because Myron needed him, so Brute had his back. Loyalty in the club was a unique symbiosis of need and a soul-deep bond so much more than love. *My brothers*. Would they still feel the same if they knew every part of him?

For almost as long as Myron could remember, first in Chicago and then here in Fort Wayne, the clubhouse buildings were the only homes he'd known. He'd partied, broken bread with his brothers, slept...lived in the clubhouse. He'd watched crop after crop of fresh prospects roll in, get their feet under them in the life, and move out—integrating the club into their entire world. *It is my world*.

Gaze to the street ahead of them, he thought back through the houses he'd helped arrange for so many Rebel members, repeatedly matching amenities against need so successfully, it was one of the many things he was known for. Give him a list of requirements for size, location, schools, or security, and he'd find the perfect match.

What a joke. The one thing he'd never been able to find for himself. He'd never felt the loss before, never had a driving need for a space of his own. Once in a blue moon, he'd rent something, but then he'd realize he spent four out of five nights at the clubhouse, so it seemed a waste.

All those houses, and none for him. Bones' place probably felt the most like a home, probably because Ester was there.

Andy's house had felt comfortable from the moment Myron had stumbled in. They'd passed the babysitter on the driveway, her amused, "Have a good night, Mr. Kasmouski," chasing them up the walk and through the doorway. Then, Myron had literally tripped over the threshold because Andy, who had been leading, had turned and gripped the edges of Myron's cut, pulling hard.

The door slipped closed, shutting out the world and closing him in with Mouse. Pressed together from hips to shoulders, Myron didn't resist when Mouse shoved him against the wall. Lips to Myron's ear, Mouse told him he'd read everything Myron needed. "I've got you, remember that. You like it a little dirty, I've got that for you, too."

"God, please." The words were slurred, letters stumbling over his teeth in their hurry to get out. He wanted Mouse to keep doing exactly what he was doing, but he also wanted more. "I need." A breath followed by a groan. "Please."

"I know what you need. You need this." Hot mouth working down his neck, Mouse shoved at Myron's cut. He caught it at the last moment, kept it from hitting the floor and draped it across a table by the entry. Myron slipped his hands under Mouse's shirt, dragging it from his waistband so he could get at skin. "You need me." He needed to get his hands on Mouse right now, the steadying feel of hard muscles under his palms. Mouse bit his shoulder, worrying at the place where his neck connected, and Myron gasped. "Feel good, babe? I got you." Mouse's hands kept up their magic, forcing Myron's arms up to rip his shirt off over his head. Then Mouse's mouth moved across his chest, tongue and teeth working his nipple until it was puffy, so sensitive each gust of breath drifting across his skin was a riot of sensation.

"Bedroom?" He barely got that out, but the flickering memory of the babysitter meant there was a kid or maybe kids somewhere in the house, and Myron

didn't want to be the reason Mouse had some awkward explaining to do.

"Oh, yeah. Let's take this private." With Myron's shirt flipped over one shoulder, Mouse backed down the hallway, tugging Myron's waistband, jeans somehow unfastened and sagging around his hips. "So hot, I can't wait to lick every inch of you." Myron followed him, turned into a dark room when Mouse did, chasing him like a moth to a flame, mouths fused together. The door closed, and Mouse pushed him against the firm surface, chill of the wood behind Myron's shoulders while his front was molten from the feel of Mouse's chest against his.

Mouse kissed as if he'd been told he would never have another chance, licking and sipping from Myron's mouth one moment, then devouring him the next. Their tongues tangled, and Myron moaned when Mouse thrust into his mouth, sounds of each caress intimate and obscene in the same breath. Gasps mixed with groans as one of them discovered a sensitive spot, the rustle of clothing being discarded. Mouse turned him, still kissing, hands still roaming, and Myron shuffled, hobbled by his jeans. Then he was falling backwards, Mouse following him down to the mattress, landing on him like a heavy blanket he could lie under for a decade.

He lost Mouse's heat, then took the opportunity to make quick work of kicking his boots off, wanting more of this thing he'd denied himself for so long. So many fears cast aside in this moment, their movements as synchronized as if they'd been lovers for years. Naked, he arched against Mouse, dick so hard it ached, every graze of Mouse's legs against his a prickly pleasure.

"Slow, babe." Mouse ripped his mouth away and shoved his face against Myron's neck. "I'm gonna blow you keep that up."

"Mouse, please."

A hand slipped down his chest, fingertips tweaking a nipple hard enough to make him gasp before continuing its path. "I know what you need." Fingers circled his bellybutton, teased and tickled for a moment before curving around his waist and gripping his cheek. "You need this." Pulling Myron up as he thrust down, the first glide of Mouse's cock against his hip was overshadowed by the request. Voice softer, less severe, Mouse invited Myron to call him by Andy. Demanded it, really, and the knowledge that Andy was exposing that part of himself was thrilling.

He'd immediately echoed it, "Andy, please."

"Please, what?"

Teeth grazed his earlobe as fingers gripped his ass hard, pulling him up and into Andy's body. His hips thrust up, cock seeking more of that slick contact, a warm puddle of liquid pooling on his belly. "More, Andy."

"More? What more? Want me to fuck you?"

He tensed, muscles going rigid at unwelcome memories that crowded in hard and fast. Pain and shame washed over him like a cold wave, and with an *inarticulate noise, he pushed hard at Andy's chest, trying to gain distance between them.*

"No, babe. Stop." Andy didn't let him go, arms wrapping around Myron's shoulders and holding him in place. The last place Myron wanted to be right now.

"Let go," Myron growled, getting his elbow between them and shoving harder, slipping a few inches across the bed. Andy threw a leg over Myron's hips, the sensation of coarse hair rough and almost too much against the head of his weeping cock. A cock that hadn't gotten the news yet that its owner was done with this scene.

"Stop it. I didn't mean...not anal. We don't have to...that's not what I meant, Myron." He rocked his hips, and Myron felt Andy's dick slip past his hip, gliding across his belly to nudge his still rigid cock. "I mean like this, this is fucking too, babe." Andy didn't release him, instead pulling Myron up again and rolling them so their cocks made better contact. "Stay with me, babe. Lemme do this for you. Make you feel good. Don't go." Andy leaned over and kissed him, teasing with flicks of his tongue. "Stay."

It took minutes of soft words and softer touches, Andy's hand slipping up and down Myron's spine, soothing the tension away, but eventually, Myron relaxed into Andy's hold again. The quiet patter of encouragement that filled the air around them was slowly replaced with the more sensuous sounds of bodies moving together. More carefully, but no less intently, Andy set a rhythm of pushing and arching, their cocks sword fighting between them, glancing off the other with each brief contact causing electric sparks to rush up and down Myron's spine.

Andy's quiet approval freed Myron of his fears, finally, and he reached between them to wrap his hand around their cocks, lining them up as he rocked his hips in time to Andy's movements. Each sensation was amplified by Andy's mouth at his neck, the praise Andy fed him like candy, whetting his appetite for more sweet words. Dirty talk seemed to come easily to Andy and thank God, he wasn't daunted by silence from his partner, but deep satisfaction was clear in his tone when he managed to drive a moaned plea out of Myron again.

It felt good. Hell, it just was *good, but Myron wanted...that ineffable "more" he'd had at the beginning, before his memories freaked him out. He rolled, wordlessly tugging at Andy until the man got on board with the idea and shifted, stretching out on top of Myron. Within moments, Myron was buried in sensation again. Heat and weight all over him, limbs restricted by Andy's hold made his breath come fast and shallow, huffing against Andy's chest and neck.*

Andy's mouth had more freedom in this position, and he took advantage of it in a way Myron loved, tipping his chin up to give better access. Andy sprawled on top of him, hips still working in time but now Myron had the weight and friction of rutting up against the body above him. Solid and masculine, fur-covered and absolutely, unmistakably male. So perfect for me. Everything I want. *Andy propped himself on a forearm and slipped his hand between them, his fingers joining Myron's around their* cocks. He urged a rougher hold, groaning into Myron's mouth when he complied, the heads of their cocks bumping across the ridges of his fingers.

Andy's dick was shorter than Myron's, but what it lacked in length it made up for in width. Broad, his cockhead had mushroomed out and Myron slicked his thumb across the slit, dragging a gasp out of Andy that made him feel a hundred feet tall. He did it again, then jacked them both harder, pulling his hand up and down with a harsh grip Andy seemed to like if the sounds pouring from his mouth were any indication. Gasping and whining, he cried, "I'm close."

Myron licked a path along Andy's shoulder to the soft flesh of his neck, and after a moment of hesitation, sank his teeth in briefly, the quick shudder of Andy's body proof he'd been right to follow his instincts. Andy liked it a little rough. So do I, apparently. "Me, too." He grunted, straining as he arched up. "Close."

"Fuck, babe. So good." Andy's mouth was next to Myron's ear, audible breaths broken by deep grunts. "Now. God, coming. Babe."

The first splash of heat on his belly was enough to tip him over the edge, and Myron found himself writhing under Andy, rutting against his belly, hands full of the sheets he had ripped off the bed. He held on while Andy wrapped him up, giving Myron his full weight, letting Myron thrust and push until he came so hard it felt like a bomb detonated at the base of his spine. Long moments of gentle strokes from Andy's fingers across his ribs and back, anchored him until the orgasm rolled away, leaving *him feeling like his skin was too small, scoured raw by the sensation.*

Bright lights brought him out of the memory, and Myron saw they were parking in the hospital lot.

"We're here." Brute shoved the keys across the cab, and Myron accepted them, pushing them deep into his pocket, discreetly adjusting himself at the same time. "Call if you need us, brother. Tell Mouse we're all rooting for his girl."

The right move
Myron

The lights inside seemed just as blindingly bright as the ones in the parking lot, and Myron fought the urge to shield his eyes, narrowing them instead. He followed Andy's directions and within a few minutes, found himself in the hallway outside the designated waiting room. Through the doorway, he spied Andy in a chair, head tipped forwards. Hands clasped between his knees, he seemed to be staring at the floor, but the moment Myron entered the room he looked up as if he'd been waiting.

They met in the middle of the room, and a momentary relief that none of the Rebels had demanded to accompany him rocketed through his brain. But then Andy's arms were around him, and Myron hadn't stopped himself from returning the embrace even though there were other people in the room. He wrapped himself around Andy, cupping the back of his head to hold him closer still.

"You came." The disbelieving words preceded a series of wracking shudders, Andy's frame shaking with palpable anguish and suddenly Myron's heart was in his throat. *Jesus, is she...am I too late?*

"I came," he agreed softly. *Please, God*. He willed there to be no bad news. *Please*. He'd only met her the once, but after talking and playing with her for an hour, he'd been in love. Natalya had stolen his heart, something he hadn't believed possible. All he could do was reassure. "I'm here. Promise. I'll be here." There was no way the radiance that was Andy's little girl could be gone. Andy's stories of her antics had been the highlights of so many days. She was brilliant, and sweet, and so loved. *It'll break him*. Keeping his voice positive, he asked, "Tell me. What do you know?"

"Nothing," Andy said, words spit out as if they were bitter on his tongue. "They took her back to surgery and promised to keep me updated, but no one has come and told me anything. That was over an hour ago." Andy took a series of deep sighs, slowing his breathing until he arched against Myron's arms, leaning back. They were staring into each other's eyes, and Myron realized they were almost the same height. In his mind, his memories of their encounters, Andy always seemed so certain of himself, so confident; he'd seemed so much larger. His presence commanding. *Maybe it was because I needed him, and now, he needs me.*

"What happened?" He shifted towards the chairs, and Andy clutched at Myron's arms, coming with him in a way that said he needed the contact even more than he'd let on. Myron wrapped his hand around Andy's, holding tight. Guiding him to a seat, Myron settled Andy and then sat beside him, hand on his forearm. The muscles under his palm rippled repeatedly, and Myron looked down to see Andy making a fist, over and over. He stroked Andy's arm, waiting until Andy had begun to relax to ask, "Why'd you have to bring Talya in?"

Through the story, he steadily held Andy's gaze, listening without interruption. When he finished, Andy seemed to deflate, sagging until he came to rest against Myron. They sat like that for a moment, and Myron relished the warmth in his chest knowing Andy needed him. Then, as it always did, Myron's brain kicked into gear, looking for a way to help in a tangible way. *Maybe I can get info for him, learn how Talya is.* "I know some folks, okay? Lemme see what I can find out." Andy's expression lit up, and Myron struggled against the need to touch his face. *Not here, not in public.* "Lemme make a call." This was what Myron did best, pulling together data and facts from sources that might be unwilling, but he'd be entirely willing to lean on whoever he needed, if it would get Andy what he needed.

He started with Bulldog, securing a promise that the man would make his own calls and get back to Myron quickly. His next call was to Goose, because as an EMT, he had his own medical connections. Another promise to reach out, another promise to let Myron know as soon as anything broke loose. Carefully untangling himself from a silently resistant Andy, Myron left him in the waiting room to troll a path down to the nurses' station. Enough of them knew men in the club, so it was no surprise he found one willing to gossip a little about their young charge. Still in surgery, they were having problems keeping her stable. She'd lost a lot of blood.

Fuck.

On his way back to the waiting room, Myron went out on a limb and called DeeDee, basically Slate's mother-in-law. If the club had a matriarch, she'd be it, having been associated with the club for decades. She promised to contact the women and organize a blood drive. If Talya had needed as many transfusions as the nurse had indicated, it was one way the club could help.

As he was walking back into the waiting room, he saw an exhausted-looking doctor walk through the double doors of the surgical suite and into the hallway. Myron moved faster. Andy was the only one in the waiting room; it had to be news about Talya. The doctor paused a moment and swiped the surgical cap from his head, using the brightly colored fabric to scrub across his face. He took in a visibly deep breath, set his shoulders and stepped through the door just ahead of Myron. "Danfort family?"

Myron relaxed for a moment at the unfamiliar name. But, he saw Andy stiffen and stand, staring at the doctor with wide eyes. *Danfort?* Shaking off his confusion, he made it to Andy's side to stand shoulder-to-shoulder, propping him up as best he could as they waited for whatever pronouncement the surgeon would make.

The surgeon's voice was rough and tired as he questioned, "You're Natalya's father?"

"Yes. God, yes." Andy's response was immediate. "How is she? My little girl? She's okay?"

Natalya Danfort, not Kasmouski? What the hell?

The doctor confirmed, "She's stable and in recovery. From there she'll go to ICU."

Air rushed out of Andy, and he sagged against Myron. "She's really okay? Talya's gonna be okay?"

"It was a difficult procedure, but she's a fighter." After a more thorough explanation of the surgery, the doctor stuck his hand out, and Andy accepted, their hands moving up and down, his confidence reassuring. "I'll check back in on her soon." He released Andy and reached for Myron's hand. Startled, he instinctively gripped and shook. "If you want, the two of you can see her for a few minutes before we move her." The surgeon smiled, tired but clearly pleased he could pass along good news. "She was asking for her daddy and papa."

Andy's flinch and abbreviated denial of "He's not..." came at the same time Myron dropped the man's hand as if it burned him, stuttering, "No, I'm just...just a friend."

Andy leaned against Myron's shoulder, focus still on the doctor. "Her...Roger's dead."

There was silence for a moment, the weight of that knowledge flattening Myron. The anonymous man in the picture was no longer anonymous, he had a name. *Roger*. This explained so much. *Dead*. Andy's quiet apology and Talya's sadness. How Andy had seemed about to say something a dozen times, but Myron knew he'd held back. *Fuck*.

The doctor shook his head and then repeated himself, interrupting Myron's thoughts as he spoke to Andy, "You can see her for a few minutes. I'll take you to her." Andy stepped away, walking out of the room with a quick glance back.

Suddenly at loose ends, Myron sat as he struggled whether to stay or go. He had been blindsided by the surgeon's statement, and then floored by what Andy revealed. After remembering Talya's "That's Daddy's seat" and now learning her name was Danfort, he knew it shouldn't have been such a shock. He knew the man in the picture was important...had been important to Andy and his daughter. *I just didn't want to believe. Things with Andy felt real.* A montage running through his head, every encounter looked different studied through the lens of this knowledge.

Stay, or go.

His heart and head were at war, bile twisting up the back of his throat when his imagination painted a scene of the man in that picture bursting into the waiting room, demanding to see his little girl. Myron imagined a tearful bedside reunion in full-color detail, him standing to the side, forgotten. That had to be what Andy would prefer.

No wonder he seems reserved sometimes, and pushing forwards at a hundred miles an hour at others.

The memory of Andy's voice and tight hold finally decided him, convincing him to stay exactly where he was. If Talya's *Daddy* was dead, then Andy would need someone to help support him and his daughter during a time like this, and Myron believed Andy deserved to have whoever he wanted. *I want to be that.*

Myron shoved down his negative thoughts, turning back to his phone and working on various non-critical club projects. So many times his role in the club was akin to herding cats, as if his invisible fingers could be set against the edges of plates to keep everything spinning.

Noise at the door to the waiting area captured his attention and Myron looked up to see DeeDee and her old man, Jase, walking in. They were followed by Goose and Francine, then Brute and Bexley. Five more people affiliated with the club than he'd expected. *Damn.*

Over the past couple of years, a lot of his friends had coupled up. It was one thing to see it at a club party, where any Rebel member would only be alone by choice. Eager women lusting after patch holders in leather were a staple at their events, and any man who chose that route was only looking for a good time. These brothers and their old ladies were in it for the long haul. So it was another to be confronted by their happiness by the harsh light of the fluorescent hospital lights. If he could see them and how they felt, they'd recognize everything he wanted to keep secret. *Nowhere to hide.*

Forestalling their questions, Myron said, "She made it." The women smiled, DeeDee's eyes going misty. He took a deep breath. "Her tonsils came out last week, and the doc said when the scabbing in her throat came off it tore too deep. Hit her carotid. She nearly bled out before Andy..." He winced and corrected himself quickly. "Before Mouse got her here. They got it fixed, but she's still not out of the woods. He's back with her now."

"Oh, Myron," Bexley whispered and laid a hand on Myron's arm, not gripping, just pressing, her reassuring touch making something inside him bend nearly to breaking. "Is Mouse okay?" He nodded, not trusting his voice. *What the fuck is wrong with me?* It wasn't like the man was anything to him, not really. One night where Myron had let down his defenses, weeks ago. *Followed by a hundred conversations and kisses. I'm such a liar.*

He wouldn't let himself think about all the reasons why Andy had called *him*. They'd spoken frequently, sure, mostly on the phone. And in the backroom of the bar. And in the back seat of Andy's car. Andy had invited him for a repeat trip to his house again the first time Myron walked back into the bar, but he'd shut that shit down hard. Not knowing the truth about Roger, he had made some assumptions. *Got a lot wrong.*

The group in front of him parted, and he saw Andy walking back in, the expression on his face smoothing as he came straight to Myron. Instead of demanding a resumption of the comforting embrace from earlier, Andy turned and stood beside Myron, keeping a careful distance between them. Taking a deep breath, Andy swiped at his cheeks with both hands and lifted his chin. He seemed to survey the men and women, nodding at the ones he knew, reaching out to grip Bexley's hand as he did so. Out of everything, that single action bothered Myron, the back of his throat burning as he watched Andy reach out to Bexley for comfort, instead of to him. *Of course he did, you didn't exactly welcome him back, did you?* It didn't make sense why it would hurt, but it did.

He cleared his throat, forcing out a question. "How is she?"

Andy pinned him with a watery gaze. "She's better than I expected. So pale, she's so pale, Myron." Needing to touch him, to restore the connection between them in some way, Myron crossed the gulf of space between them and rested his hand on Andy's shoulder. He squeezed tightly, fingers digging in hard. "As long as everything stays as it is now, she'll be fine. They're putting her in ICU because someone can be with her all the time." Goose made a sound and Andy shook his head. "No, I know not me, not all the time. But, family," he leaned towards Myron, a sway really, their bodies nearly brushing before Andy pulled himself back upright, "and close friends can go in every couple of hours, two at a time."

It grew quiet in the room, and Myron imagined he felt the weight of everyone's stare, shocked when he glanced around to find only Bexley was looking at them, the others having gathered into a group off to the side.

Maybe it's still too fresh for him. Talya wasn't that old. For her to have memories of Roger, his death couldn't be too far in the past.

He was furious suddenly, so angry that his need to lash out was nearly unstoppable, chairs and phones and his brothers all likely looking targets. *I want…I need to be here for him.* Muscles tense, hands shaking, Myron slipped his hand around Andy's. The immediate crushing hold told him he'd made the right move. *I want to be what he needs.* He squeezed, offering a hopeful promise. "She's going to be fine. Back to singing in the kitchen in no time." Bexley made a sound like she'd suppressed a laugh and he glared at her, anger flaring again at her smile. Making this statement as he was, it would be the death knell for the thing that had saved his life so long ago, and he wanted her to respect that, even if she'd never really understand.

Andy's worth it.

"You want me to stay?" Andy nodded, the barest of movements, as if he were afraid of making too large a gesture.

Fuck 'em all.

Myron squeezed Andy's hand and leaned close, shoulders brushing. "Okay. You need me, I'm here."

Andy's audible sigh told Myron he'd again made the right decision.

Going home
Andy

He woke with a jerk, yanked out of a bloody nightmare with welcome pressure from a now-familiar hand on his shoulder. Blinking up blearily, he stared at the face hovering over him. *Myron*. Beautiful, kissable Myron. Reaching up, he wrapped his hand around the back of Myron's neck and tugged him down. When their lips met in a soft caress, the spark he anticipated leapt between them, heat flaring in his groin at the rough slide of whiskers on his skin. "Babe," he whispered, releasing his hold and moving to sit upright. He'd been dozing sprawled out across three chairs, Myron's bundled leather jacket his pillow.

Myron's eyes warmed, and the corners of his lips tipped up. "Doc's here, says he's got good news." Andy peered around him to see the surgeon standing near the doorway, phone in hand, studiously not looking their direction.

"I'm up," he said, pushing to his feet and listing sideways until Myron's hand cupped his elbow, steadying Andy. *Like he's done since he got here.* That was three days ago. Endless days filled with brief visits to Talya's bedside, vats of bad coffee, and a bellyful of fear. If it hadn't been for Myron's friends, they would have starved. *They* because Myron hadn't left the hospital, either, staying by Andy's side through everything. Even when the bleeding started again that first night, Myron hadn't panicked, just punched the button to call a nurse and ripped the door open, shouting for help while Andy cradled Talya in his arms.

A second round in the surgical suite meant Talya had spent another two days in ICU. She had finally been cleared to be put into a regular room last night, but none were available. That meant she was still parked in ICU, and they were out here except for fifteen minutes every two hours.

"I'm releasing Natalya."

Andy blinked. "What?" Myron's fingers squeezed his elbow, and he leaned sideways, resting his shoulder against Myron's solid frame. *My rock.* "Releasing, like to go home?"

"Yes, she's recovering nicely and with healing well underway, I think the calmer environment at home would be more beneficial now. I'll write the orders now, and you'll be ready to head out in about an hour."

"I'm going to...she's coming home? Really?" A thousand thoughts ran through his mind, but all he could think of was this same surgeon telling him the *same* thing just over a week ago. *"She can go home now, Mr. Kasmouski. Just convince her to take it easy. She seems like a handful."* Patent lies, because look where they were right now. *She nearly died.* Andy's throat tightened with fear, muting his hundreds of questions.

"She'll need someone with her, of course, and you'll want to follow-up with her regular pediatrician on Monday." Andy stared, mouth still stubbornly sealed shut. "She's healing well, and home is the best place for her, Mr. Kasmouski." The surgeon flashed a smile and turned, walking out of sight down the hallway.

"It's a good thing." Myron's voice rumbled in his ear, and Andy twisted his neck, meeting his gaze. "It is, Andy. She's going to be fine." Somehow when Myron said it, Andy could finally believe the words.

"I get to take her home." Terror made his voice high and wispy, and he watched Myron's expression soften in response.

"Yeah. Talya'll be excited to sleep in her own bed." Myron's hand wrapped around his and Andy held on tight, as he did every time. "I think the novelty of the hospital bed wore off a couple of days ago."

"Come home with us." He blurted the words, less of a question and more a demand, and snapped his mouth shut immediately. "I mean...I'm just..." His voice trailed off as chin down, he studied the pattern of the waiting

83

room carpet, tracing memorized lines back and forth. "What if it happens again?"

"It's not gonna happen." Myron's words were as firm as the wall the man erected between them whenever any of his friends were around. Sturdy and composed, he'd not given one single indication that being here meant to him what it did Andy. *But he's here.* That's what he kept telling himself. Myron was here, and he'd been here since Andy called. *He came.*

"What if it does?" He just couldn't shake the fear. He repeated his thoughts, sharing them in a whisper, "She almost died, Myron."

"But, she didn't." Myron leaned closer, and Andy felt the heat from his hand as it skimmed up his arm, coming to rest against the side of his neck. "She won't." Myron shook him gently, that tiny knowing smile staying in place the whole time. "She's going to be fine, Andy."

He stared into Myron's eyes, willing him to understand how terrifying it was to be alone in this. To be the sole person responsible for such a precious human being. *Please.* Myron used his hold on Andy's neck to pull him closer, resting their foreheads together. *Please don't leave me alone.*

"I'll follow you home. Stick around for a bit, if that's what you need. We're friends." That drove a startling dagger through Andy's gut. It was unexpected, and after Myron's presence through this, seemed to minimize what Andy felt. Myron's gaze locked on Andy's, eyes searching. After a moment, the corners of his mouth tilted up, and Myron shook his head. His next words set Andy's world back to rights, laying the foundation for something more. "But that's not why. I wanna be with you not because you need me, but because I want to be what you need."

Andy nodded and took a shuddering breath. Myron's hair brushed against the side of his face like a caress. They stood like that for a moment until Myron broke the stillness by angling his head forwards, lips brushing across Andy's. *God.*

"I do need you. Thank you." *I could kiss you again right now, right here.* The impulse was overwhelming, and as if he read Andy's intent, Myron broke away, pulling his ever-present phone from the front pocket of his jeans. He understood why when he heard booming laughter in the hallway, and recognized the voice of one of Myron's friends. *Of course, they can't really know.* It didn't matter that most had already guessed. As long as they kept the PDA to a minimum in front of his friends, Myron could continue to deny anything was happening between them. A sharp pain bloomed in Andy's chest, and he shoved it away, tucking it into a back corner to examine later. *Talya's coming home.* He closed his eyes, letting Myron's certainty that she was going to be okay cover him like a blanket. *Myron's coming home.* "Thank you," he repeated on a whisper and, even though he didn't understand the subtext, Myron rewarded him with a crooked, sideways smile that lit up his insides in a way that didn't say friends. *I'm in so much trouble.*

Wishes and dreams
Myron

He heard the jangle of keys as the back door opened and called, "Hey there," careful to keep his voice quiet, "she's asleep." Myron twisted to look over the back of the couch towards the kitchen, waiting for his first sight of Andy. "How was work?"

This was day three of being in Andy's house, and as he ate a dinner of macaroni and cheese accompanied by cartoons earlier, it had struck Myron how domestic this was, him hanging out at home with a still recovering Talya while Andy worked his shift at the bar. *I could totally get used to this.*

Over the past couple of days, he'd let himself fall farther into the world of make believe they'd entered when he'd followed Andy's car back here. A world where he was a permanent part of their lives. A world where it was normal and expected that he'd still be up when Andy got home from work, waiting. A world unlike anything he'd ever had before. A home and partner, complete with a beautiful, little girl.

Myron shook his head sharply, trying to unseat the fantasy. *You sleep on the couch, remember?*

So far, they hadn't gone back to teasing and flirting. With things so tenuous with Talya, Andy was on guard all the time and that alone wasn't conducive to the mood. In fact, they were in a weird place. Not boyfriends, not lovers. Just friends. *And maybe because I kinda feel like a live-in babysitter?* He squashed the thought. *I don't want that*, he admitted. *I want more. Maybe I just need to show him.*

"Not bad. We were busy with an office party, which always makes the night go fast. Thanksgiving, you know?" Andy was talking as he walked into the room, barefoot which meant his shoes were lined up neatly near the door that led to the garage. Beside Myron's boots. *Domestic.* "How was she?" Andy stood near the back of the couch, looking down.

Determined to shake things up, see where they might be after this was done, Myron reached up, traced a touch down Andy's arm and threaded their fingers together. Startled, Andy blinked at him and then his expression warmed, and he dipped to press his mouth against Myron's, humming happily when Myron stroked the tip of his tongue across the seam of his lips. "Hi."

"Hi, yourself." Andy pulled back a fraction of an inch, still so close Myron felt the breath used to compose the words when he asked, "Did you eat?"

With a grin, Myron lunged up and snaked his arms around Andy's shoulders and waist. He tugged, overbalancing and pulling Andy over the back of the couch and on top of him with a muffled shout. He slid to the side at the last moment, so Andy's weight mostly hit the cushions. "She's fine." He angled an arm under Andy's neck, pulling him closer. "And yes, I ate. Did you?"

"You have something in mind for me to eat?" Andy's eyebrows waggled suggestively, and Myron chuckled. "I'm feeling a little peckish. I could—" He leaned in and nipped Myron's lobe before sucking on it. "—be convinced to nibble on *something*." Teeth grazed along his throat, and Myron arched his neck, letting Andy access the sensitive spots, groaning at the tease of a hot mouth dragging along the side of his throat. "Oh, yeah, babe. I could definitely eat."

The playful lilt to his voice jolted Myron's heart, making it thud along like a cold bike engine. *This, this right here. This is what I want.* The knowledge slotted into place with a resounding click in his head. This was everything wound round Myron's fantasies, and an unnamed heart's desire come to life. This man, a partner he could love.

What the fuck?

Andy pulled back. "What's wrong?"

Myron swallowed and forced a smile. "Nothing."
Love?

Andy studied him for a moment, eyebrows bunched together as his gaze slowly swept Myron's face. He shifted so he was more fully against the back of the couch, pushing into the cushions as he placed his hand at Myron's waist. "You know I want you here, right? You aren't just a convenience to me. Not a babysitter."

The echo of his earlier thoughts poked at him. He couldn't forget how damn smart Andy was; it wouldn't do to underestimate him. Myron blinked. "I didn't think that at all." He'd been propped up on an elbow and let it slide out from under his head slowly, putting his face on a level with Andy's. "I was somewhere else in my head."

"Where?" Andy scooted a tiny bit closer, but still not the full-body contact Myron needed.

Do I tell him? He could either come clean or spin a yarn. *Is this a possibility for me? Can I have...him?* "This..." His voice trailed off, and Andy scooted closer, thighs pressing together now. "I was thinking this was something I didn't know I wanted." Andy gave a wiggle, and Myron felt the press of a hardening cock against his hip. "I never let myself dream of anything this good, because wishes and dreams aren't...productive." Fingers tugged at his shirt, and Myron lifted, letting it slide over his head and off. "You walked in and I realized if I'd let myself dream, I'd have dreamed of you."

Andy's lips pursed, the bottom lip bowing down sweetly, and he leaned closer, his hand sliding up

Myron's chest to his neck. With a tight grip, he edged closer and then his mouth was on Myron's. Unlike any of their other kisses, this one felt poignant and tender, as if Andy was reacquainting himself with something he remembered liking, teasing and touching until Myron was panting. "I'm never gonna let you go now, beautiful man." Myron nipped that bottom lip, making Andy pull in a quick breath. "I'm not kidding, Myron. I'm gonna hold you, and I won't let you forget this is your dream. Because, babe, you're my dream, too."

Myron spread his fingers across Andy's chest, curving them so his nails dug in, dragging down to his belly, knowing Andy's shirt would blunt the pain. It still drew a gasp and a shiver from the man in his arms. Andy lifted on an elbow, leaning over Myron and rocking his hips to press his hard cock against Myron's leg. He raised his chin and Andy bent to him, mouth descending to his where it took possession, owning his lips and teeth and tongue in a dance drawn together by breath and need.

Myron loved kissing Andy. Loved how into it the man could get, how lost they would be within moments of first contact. Andy sprawled on him like this sent his senses into overdrive, to a place where he heard every brush of fabric, the scrape of fingertips as they slid across skin. In the distance, he heard a little girl's cough. Andy immediately tensed and broke the kiss, pressing his forehead against Myron's.

"Come to my bedroom." Not a request, this demand left no question about what Andy wanted. Myron had stayed on the couch these past few nights, not wanting to disturb the sanctity of the master bedroom, and not certain of where he and Andy were, not enough to try and push his way into Andy's bed. Tonight, though, it felt like the right thing.

He nodded, and Andy's breath whooshed over his lips. They hadn't talked about Roger beyond a few brief words at the hospital, and there was so much for Myron to learn, but for now—this was enough.

Unka Myron

Andy

He lay on his side and watched Myron sleep, grinning at how the man spread out, arms and legs angled so he took over the whole bed. *Not that there's much bed here.* He considered the idiocy of sleeping in the guest room when there was a perfectly serviceable master, not for the first time. Other than marking it off the list of chores when he needed to go in and dust or vacuum, he ignored that space. *I hate this house.* It had been Roger's, and in so many ways remained his dead partner's home. Once past the furious activity following Roger's death, Andy never cared much to make his mark on something that he'd never wanted.

It had been a home for Talya, and a safe space where she could hold onto her memories of her daddy. But these days, when she no longer objected to Myron sitting beside Andy at the dining room table, it made

Andy think it might be time to move on. Yesterday at lunch, she'd pulled tears to Andy's eyes by patting the seat as she walked around the table, telling Myron, "Sit here, Unka Myron." *Uncle Myron, gah.* Myron had grinned broadly, playing the gentleman by helping her climb into her seat first.

We need to make a place for us.

Myron contracted his spread appendages and rolled, and Andy took the opportunity to snuggle in behind him. He wrapped his arms around Myron's chest, resting his head against one shoulder blade. *Maybe it's time?* He pressed a kiss to the back of Myron's neck, darting his tongue out to graze a quick lick across his skin, still salty. The room smelled like them, like the hot and heavy make-out session they'd had earlier. *I like that it smells like him.*

Right after Roger died, Andy had managed a few nights of unsettled sleep in the master bedroom. Once the immediate exhaustion of grief wore away, however, he found the space filled with so many emotions he wanted to avoid. He'd been overwhelmed with anger and regret, because he knew he hadn't loved Roger like he could have. *Should have.* They'd been a couple of friends who got along well enough, hearts tied together by their little princess. That was one of the things that kept tripping him up now, the feeling that this—what he had with Myron—was richer than anything he'd had with Roger. After these weeks building things with Myron, he couldn't imagine going back to the poor fare his life with Roger had been.

It was like Myron was a buffet, full of flavors and rich sauces around every corner. The way the man took care of Andy and Talya was humbling. He'd essentially moved in, not because Andy had asked him, but because he saw a need. Slept on the couch until tonight, when Andy had woken from his freak-out haze and finally asked. Myron hadn't pushed, just made sure Andy and Talya were taken care of. Sure, Andy could have arranged care for Talya, piecing shifts-worth of coverage that would get them by until she could go back to school. That hadn't been enough for Myron though, so he'd gone all in, even having some of his friends do basic shopping for them. Andy had come home to a truck and two bikes in the driveway that first night, rushing inside with his heart in his throat to find them packing away the last of the groceries. Myron had seen a need and worked to fill it. *He's gonna keep doing that for me...for us.*

Myron shifted, and Andy moved with him, loving how all of Myron's muscles and strength were subdued by sleep, like he was recharging by resting here in bed with him. Myron was always on the move, always busy, so seeing him like this was a luxury. *I can have this every night.* He readjusted, draping himself all along Myron's back, grinning to himself when Myron's ass wiggled backwards, seeking contact even in his sleep.

It's time, was his last thought before sleep claimed him.

***

Myron

"Can we talk?" Andy's words surprised Myron and he twisted to see him standing in the kitchen doorway. It was Talya's first day back at school, and they hadn't discussed it, but Myron knew his time here was winding down.

One week, with four glorious nights sleeping beside this man. *Well, not so much sleeping.* He wasn't looking forwards to rejoining the rest of the world, and that was exactly what this talk signaled. Still, it would be good to know where things stood between them.

"Okay," he said easily and turned, dropping the dishrag over the divider between the sinks.

Andy strolled towards him, only stopping when he was close enough to touch. He reached out and hooked a finger in Myron's pocket, tugging so his back arched and hips pressed into Andy's.

"I hate this house." Myron blinked, surprised and unable to find any words to use for a response. Andy continued, "I want to tell you why." Okay, that made more sense.

Andy slipped his hand down to Myron's, fingers threading through as he tugged, leading Myron towards the couch in the other room. He sat and pulled Myron down beside him, waiting until everything was arranged as he wanted before he began.

"Roger was a good man." Andy sighed. "That sounds so...trite. Like something anyone would say. 'He's a good man.' But it describes him. He was. We...fell into a relationship." He sighed again. "It wasn't extraordinary.

It wasn't heaven on earth. It was good. Talya made us better together, and she loved us both."

"Did he love you?" *How in the hell will I ever measure up against a dead guy?* Myron had been dreading having this knowledge, understanding who Andy had been attracted to before. Maybe that was why he'd been okay with not talking about it.

"I'd like to think he did, but I don't know." Eyes narrowed, Myron studied Andy.

He was serious. That man, the Roger who had shared a life and a daughter with Andy, may have been good, but it definitely hadn't been good enough. Carefully Myron said, "If you love someone, you tend to let them know."

Andy shifted beside him and Myron felt a touch on his chin, Andy's fingers turning his face so they stared at the other. They sat like that for a moment, uncertainty stirring Myron's insides.

"You're right. If you love someone, your actions speak for you, even if your words don't." A soft touch brushed across Myron's lips, then back again, mesmerizing in its regularity. "Like being ready to out yourself because they need you."

"I don't—" Andy's thumb pressed against his lips, halting his words. *I don't love him.* His insides gave that quiver again from earlier. *Do I?*

"There's a lot I want to say. About Roger. This house." Andy leaned in, fingers holding Myron's chin steady as he placed a series of soft kisses on his lips. The rasp of scruff against his lips and chin had Myron's cock waking up. Sitting beside him like this, so close he was nearly on Andy's lap, it reminded him of how it felt to be wrapped up by Andy. Weight and pressure, arms and hands holding him tight, all he could do was take in air, and even that was laced with Andy's scent. "And about us. All of it good."

Myron let the silence build between them for a few seconds, willing his erection away as he waited. Then he took a breath, centered himself as he would when approaching a negotiation with another club, and said, "Tell me what you want me to know." The rest could wait.

They had time.

The right guy
Myron

"I like it." He stood in the empty living room, already envisioning how it would look filled with the comfortable, slouchy, kid-friendly furniture he had in mind. The real estate agent, the older sister to one of their long-time members, Tequila, grinned up at him. He rolled his eyes. "Yes, Dianita. I'm going to buy it if we can come to an agreement."

She grinned fiercely. "I knew it." Offering a high five, she said, "Oh, we'll come to an agreement. The sellers are motivated. When you told me what you wanted and the timeframe, and as always, your demands were so detailed, I knew it had to be this one."

Four bedrooms, three baths, living and den spaces, and a huge backyard. In Talya's school district. *Yeah, Dianita came through again.* He walked up the hallway towards the master suite, pausing in the doorway. *This is stupid*. Andy had texted him earlier asking about dinner. He was off tonight and would be cooking. *Domestic*. He looked around the room again. *I'll put light-colored wood in here, with some bright accents*. "Dianita, I want painters before I have furniture delivered. I'll get you some swatches of what I want."

"What?" He heard her coming towards him but didn't turn around, fascinated with his detailed vision of Andy in this room. "Is this for you, Myron?" Without looking at her, he nodded. She huffed a laugh, then asked, "You're moving to Fort Wayne?"

"Looks like it." *I need to talk to Mason*. "Make an offer, twenty-five below asking, since I'll be paying cash." *Make sure he'll be cool with it*. That wasn't really a concern because Myron had watched how the club had bent around member's needs before. At her intake of breath at his demand, he shook his head trying to stop her argument. "They won't accept it, I know. But it's a good place to start." The house was already priced reasonably because the previous owners were liquidating as part of a divorce. He wouldn't rake them over the coals, but he would drive a bargain. "I want to close in a week." The inspection and title search had already been done, and without the need to organize a loan, he could move fast. "I want to be moved in by the week before Christmas, Dianita. Make it happen."

"Holy shit." She snorted, and he turned to look at her, grinning at the twist of her mouth. He knew her, had worked with her on so many deals, he knew what that meant. "You know how I do love a challenge."

"That I do." He pushed past her to the hallway and turned, walking past the guest room and through the living space into the other wing. There were two bedrooms on this end of the house, connected by a large Jack-and-Jill bathroom. He opened the door to the larger of the two bedrooms. "I might need some help with this one." Dianita had followed him, and he heard a questioning noise. "Other than pink and purple, what do six-year-old girls like?"

"Oh, honey." Her voice was soft. "I can help with that."

An hour later, he was in the office at the clubhouse, computer on the desk in front of him. Bank website open on the screen, he was moving money between his personal accounts. Years of shrewd investments meant he would not only be able to purchase the house cash, but also could afford to furnish it as he wanted. He studied the balances and grinned. *With plenty left over.*

His phone buzzed against his leg, and he pulled it out, seeing Bones contact information on the screen. He used his thumbprint to accept the call through the secure app the club used, and the video image of Bones popped onto the screen. "Hey, Bones. What's up?"

"Ester wanted to ask you when you will return to Chicago."

Myron smiled. "She's still not using the phone, huh?"

"She is not. That remains an insurmountable obstacle for her." Bones stared at him, the tattoos on the man's face not even worth Myron's attention these days. The man was a friend and brother, and like the club, had been part of his life since Mason plucked Myron out of the shelter. That he'd met and wooed Myron's sister, also homeless, and lost to him for so long, that was just fate pulling tricks by crossing the life threads of people who meant something to him. "That was not an answer, Myron."

"No, it wasn't. I don't know when I'll be back." He really should talk to Mason first, but Bones and Ester deserved to know, too. *She's my sister, dammit*. Decision made, he committed himself to the move in a public way, hoping it wouldn't blow up in his face. "I'm moving to Fort Wayne. I bought a house here this morning."

Bones looked startled, eyes widening. Ester's voice came from a distance away, and the video shifted, swinging drunkenly around as Bones turned the phone to face Myron's sister. "My Ronnie. No. Settling your new past findings in my head aren't done yet. Memory making needs to happen more, please." She looked stricken, her face paling as she stared at the phone.

"I'm not far, honey. Promise. I'll be back more often than you want."

"Distruth. I want you for the always that we never had." Ester's brain was wired differently, one of the things Bones seemed to love about her. Myron knew it was just his own quirks echoed in magnified ways in his sister. "You're the everything I'll have for family, like

101

Bones is the everything I'll need for living." The expression on her face was pain, raw and real. "Always is most with more love."

"We have always, my sissy. Promise you." He held her gaze through the screen. "You're the busy one these days, with your volunteering at the shelter. Gunny told me you're doing great work with the rescued dogs. I understand you're gonna be busy for weeks, maybe longer. All those pups need love." By mentioning the dogs, he carefully skirted her mention of the knowledge that had sent her into a depression so deep it had taken rehabbing abused dogs to pull her out of it.

She wanted children with a fierce need, but events of her childhood made that impossible. A dream she could never realize. When they found out, she'd been so devastated by the knowledge, Bones had reached out to the members of the club in fear, desperate to find something to pull her out of her own head.

Gunny had come through for her, using his connections to find a mission in which she could immerse herself. The Cook County sheriff department had raided a dogfighting compound and seized nearly four dozen dogs. A number of the animals had to be put down, but the remainder were being trained to enter a brand-new life as a pet. Ester had made a huge impression with how well she'd connected with the dogs. So much so, the shelter had wanted to recognize her at a dinner last month. Needless to say, that was a non-starter, but Gunny had been pleased to accept on her behalf.

"I want you here." Her bottom lip pouted down, and he thought she looked as adorable as Talya had when he put her to bed last night. "Please. My Ronnie."

"My new house has a guest room. The door locks from inside." Her head tipped to the side. "I've got a big backyard, too. Even though it's winter, I saw lots of birds around." Her head tipped to the other side. Myron gave her a final incentive. "I'm closer to where Willa is with Gar and Dolly." He knew he had her then, because she loved Mason's wife and children, loved all the Rebel kids, really. Kids were easier for her to deal with because they were mostly honest about how they felt, something Ester could get behind. She found the adult world exhausting. "You can come visit any time Bones will bring you down."

"Will you take me?" She stared past the phone now, and he knew she'd focused on Bones. "Yay." Gaze back to Myron, she frowned. "I'm not happiest, but even a little of the happy is better than sad."

"Yeah, sissy. Happy is better than sad." He blew her a kiss, and she grabbed at air, clutching her clenched fist tight to her chest. "Love you, Ester. I'll see you." She smiled, and the video shifted again, Bones' face filling the screen. "Thanks, Bones."

"As always, you are entertaining, if nothing else." Bones nodded. "Be safe, brother."

"Shiny side," Myron agreed. The video call ended, and he laid the phone down with a sigh.

"Moving to the Fort, huh?" Mason's voice came from the doorway, and Myron looked up with a grin. "Plannin' on tellin' me at some point?"

"Hey, Mason, I'm moving to Fort Wayne in the next couple of weeks, but I can continue to work on whatever you need me to out of Chicago."

There was a moment of silence, then a heavy sigh. "Most members petition to change chapters." Mason settled on the couch along the wall. "Most members would rather move towards Mother, than away." Chicago was where the club had been founded, and all members of the main central chapter sported rockers proudly proclaiming their assignment. "I'd be okay if you wanted to keep that rocker, brother. What's got you moving down here?"

This was it, the chance he'd hoped for. Mason hadn't been at the hospital, but Myron knew he had to have heard the stories. *Time to come clean.*

"You know how you're always telling me to find what makes me happy and hold tight to that?" Mason nodded. "I found it here."

"Your bartender?" It was Myron's turn to nod. Mason's tone was even when he said, "I figured as much. You gonna be okay with the shit that comes with this? There's a fuckton of shit gonna rain on you from some of the brothers."

"If you think I'm a distraction because of what...because of who I'm with, I'll figure something out.

I won't put the club at risk, you know me better than that."

Mason shook his head, leaning forwards to put his elbows on his knees. Hands dangling between his legs, he frowned, brows pulling together above suddenly serious eyes. "Not where I was takin' that at all. You're valued, and I appreciate every single fuckin' thing you've done for the club. But, brother, you've let a lot of the men believe you chased tail. Professional, exclusive, high-class, celebrity...I've heard all kinds of speculation through the years. Each stretch of the story taking it farther. There's going to be a bunch of our men who aren't any more surprised than I am. But the ones who didn't figure it out are going to be crowing over you finally settling down. That's the shit I mean, Myron. Don't matter the gender, not in my club."

"Not true, and you know it." This was why he'd been so quiet and discrete through the years, scarcely ever believing the risks of being found out were worth hurried, unsatisfying encounters. "And the clubs we deal with, they'll be worse. Situations like today, the day will come when you may not want me at your table anymore."

A support club in Fort Wayne had gotten caught up in a mess, the leadership's ambition overstretching their abilities by a far mark. Slate had caught word that they were planning on double-crossing the Rebels, and based on the legal activities happening right now at their tiny clubhouse on the west side of town, that word was correct. Myron had been monitoring the state of affairs all day, trying to determine when, or even if, the Rebels might need to step in and do damage control. So far, so good, but it was still an active situation. Eventually the Rebels would have to make an example about the bad decisions the club had made. For today, however, things were controlled.

"Fuck that noise." Mason's tone was so firm Myron blinked. "You? Brother, you can fuck who you want. Long as it doesn't get in the way of anything else *you* wanna do, who gives a flyin' fuck? Jesus, My, don't you get it? The club isn't anything without the men who live and breathe it. Men who live free, support their brothers and families, men the club can get behind if we're needed, because there's a mutual trust. Trust, brother. You're one of those trusted few. Don't let shit get twisted up in your goddamned head."

"Hard not to when I know I'm right." Myron pushed back from the desk. "Not having me sit in on meetings, that's me just putting it out there as an option in case it's needed. Just admit you need to think on it."

"Wanna ask you something." Mason paused until Myron nodded. "When's the last time you heard us raggin' on gays?" Mason's hands were clasped in front of his face, one finger against his lips, the position a sure indication of how serious he was. "Sure, a decade ago. But that was before I figured some shit out. Before a lot of us figured shit out. Tequila's old lady, you know her, right?" Myron nodded. "Fifteen years ago, you ever think a brother would be latching onto a woman of color, no matter how class she was?" Without giving Myron a chance to respond, he kept going. "Course not, but fuckin' times have changed, brother. How many support clubs we got that are mixed? Fuck, Myron, *we're* mixed. We got white, black, brown of every shade...fuck, as far as I know, we don't got no yellow, but that's not because we'd give a shit." Mason pushed to his feet. "Why in the fuck would you think I'd give a shit you were gay?" He took the two steps to the door and turned to glare back at Myron. "Now you give *that* a fuckin' think, you hear me?"

"I hear you, boss." Mason's words had shaken him, because if he were right—and face it, Mason was nearly always right—then Myron might always have been the only thing holding himself back. *Maybe it took meeting the right guy.* On cue, his phone buzzed, and he looked down to see a regular call. Andy.

"Hi." He could hear the smile in his voice, and that just made him grin harder. The voice that came through the phone didn't echo his pleasure, and the words wiped the smile off his face.

"Myron, we need to talk."

What did you do
Andy

He sat and stared fixedly at the kitchen door, knee popping up and down as his bare heel beat a tattoo against the floor. Mother Danfort had picked up Talya, asking no questions about his panicked call for help. He just knew he needed to get Talya out of the house for this. *How did I not know?* It was lightly snowing outside so he was surprised to hear a bike approaching. That was followed a minute later by a knock at the front door. *What the hell?* Myron had a key; Andy didn't know why he would knock.

Maybe it's not Myron. Sudden fear drove him to his feet, and he hurried to the door, yanked it open without looking through the peephole to see...Myron. Pent-up breath released in relief, he leaned forwards for the expected welcoming kiss only to find nothing but cold air as Myron swayed backwards, just out of reach.

"Hey," he said softly, studying Myron for an indication of what was going on. "What's wrong?"

"You tell me." Curt, the words seemed torn from his throat, and Andy flinched at the jagged tone. "You're the one who wanted to *talk*."

Not smiling, because nothing made sense, Andy reached out and gripped Myron's arm, tugging him inside. "Yeah, we need to talk."

Myron's shoulders inched up, and he tipped his head back, blowing out a stream of air towards the ceiling. "Just tell me what's wrong. We'll sort it out." Andy couldn't help himself, reaching out to touch his chest, and Myron bent his neck, looking down at him. In his boots, with Andy in bare feet, he was a couple of inches taller. "You don't wanna know what I'm thinking." As if daring him to ask, Myron straightened and stared at him, brows arching towards his hairline.

"Come sit down." Myron glanced at the kitchen, then down the hallway towards Talya's room. "She's with her grandmother." Now Myron's gaze cut towards the table, laptop sitting beside crumpled pages from the newspaper. He eyed the mess for a moment, then looked back at Andy who'd tugged on his hand. "I need you to explain."

Myron widened his stance and crossed his arms over his chest. He hadn't taken off his jacket yet, and the leather creaked ominously. "So tell me what this is I need to explain."

"You want to come sit down?" Andy stepped back and let his hand drop. This wasn't going how he'd expected, not at all. How he'd feared, sure. Hoped, not at all. "Please?"

"What I want is to hear whatever it is you have to say." His jaw set, and Andy watched as Myron's lips pressed into a thin line. "So I can know where things are."

"I wanted to understand about your...we haven't really had a chance to talk about the club. The Rebels. There's an article in the paper and...I wanted...it just felt like I need to know some things." *Like where you stand with the things the club's accused of.* "I've heard things." He had, too. This morning, from the next door neighbor. *"Do you know what kind of trash you're letting in Roger's house?"* That had been the lead-in to an uncomfortable conversation. The man waving his paper at Andy's face, talking fast, so that the only things that penetrated were "searched" and "outlaw gang." That had driven him to make a trip to the store, buying his own paper. Doing a search online and coming up with a whole lot of information he hadn't expected.

Realizing Myron didn't plan to budge from his current position, Andy straightened his shoulders, deciding to push through from this weird place—*where things were*—and get to what he hoped would be the better plans for the evening. "Talya's my daughter."

"What? Of course, she is. You're her papa." Myron's mouth snapped shut, and Andy guessed he hadn't intended the outburst.

"Well, yeah. I am. And that means she's my responsibility." He glanced at the couch. "Are you sure you don't want to..." His words trailed off when Myron's expression didn't change, and tried to pick up the thread of the story he wanted to tell. "Roger was friends with the neighbors. One of them came over and shared"—*understatement*—"his concerns this morning. Your friends didn't make the front page, but the story wasn't buried." Myron paled, and a muscle jumped in his jaw, the contours of his neck flexing as he swallowed. "He said this wasn't the first time the club's run into trouble in town." The look on Myron's face didn't tell him anything, nothing of guilt or innocence, at least. The anger reflected there, though? That was blazingly clear. *What if it's all wrong?* Embarrassment swallowed him whole. Staring at the floor, he said, "Talya's my...I have to know she's safe. Some of the things they reported in the paper and online—" Andy grimaced, letting the horror of those memories wash through him. "Those don't always paint your friends in the best possible light. How much of what they say is true?"

"Which neighbor? Who talked to you? Jesus, Andy, do I have to defend myself against anyone who comes along with an opinion, or have you already made up your mind?"

The verbal attack jolted Andy out of his thoughts, and he looked up to see a sneer on Myron's face, his mouth twisted as if he were in pain. "What? No, it wasn't like...he's not like that. He's just looking out for Talya."

"Yeah, and I never pegged you for someone who'd throw everything you know out the door. You know me, Andy. You know me better than this."

"The paper said there was a raid. On a motorcycle gang's clubhouse. When you aren't here, you always say you're at the clubhouse. Tell me that the police weren't knocking on their door this morning. Tell me, and I'll believe you. I know you'd never hurt Talya. But your friends?" Myron's words had cut deep, and Andy struggled against showing the emotion. Myron's head shook back and forth slowly and his stubborn refusal to explain made Andy angry, and he snapped, "Jesus, she's my daughter. Don't you think I deserve at least that? To know if she's safe? To understand who you invited into Roger's house?" Myron's eyes widened, and Andy covered his mouth. *I shouldn't have said those words.* Fighting tears, he croaked, "You asked me for honesty the other night. Wanted to know what happened with Roger. I told you, Myron. Told you everything. Didn't I tell you how Roger left me, left me and Talya to fend for ourselves? How he died overseas? I wasn't even Talya's guardian. It was a near thing, with the social workers all talking like foster care would be preferable to the gay man living in her father's house. But somehow, between Mother Danfort and my grandmother, I found the help I needed so I could keep her. Keep her in her home. A home her father made for her. For us." He pulled in a breath intended to calm, but Myron's mouth insistently staying shut made him reckless. "You tell me my daughter is safe. Tell me I'm safe."

"You think...you think for a moment I'd let anything happen to Talya? To you?" Looking staggered, Myron asked for clarification. "You don't trust me to keep you safe?"

"No, I don't." It wasn't true, but he'd lost control and was lashing out. Angry and hurt, because Myron hadn't explained anything, and the news reports were very clear the kind of things the gang was into: rape, drugs, and even murder. "You're going to have to do better than that." Myron stepped forwards and stopped when Andy took a matching step backwards. "Don't. You don't get to come in here and decide what I need to know. Not when my questions are valid. Jesus, Myron. She's my daughter. So don't try to soothe me like what I'm asking doesn't matter. Not until I can understand. Not until you tell me what's going on."

"I can't, Andy. They aren't just my friends, that's...the Rebels are my family." Andy shook his head. "I pulled your story out of you hand over fist, you fighting me the whole way, because I cared enough to want to know. I understand things have been going fast, and you've had a lot on your mind, but did you ever once...just one time...did you think to ask about my life and what I might have going on? So, what? My brothers are good enough to spend money at the bar, but now you're worried about them helping keep Talya safe? Those are the best men I fucking know. They saved my life. Saved a lot of people." That last was a roar and Andy jerked backwards, stumbling over his own feet. "And you're going to stand there are tell me you're afraid of them? Of me?"

"I'm just saying that we need to talk about this—" He gestured towards the table, pointing towards what still felt like damning evidence. "—and it should be sooner rather than later."

"Yeah, you're right. After I've spent the time with you becoming invested in you, I guess it's about time you started asking about me and my life. There I was, feelin' all proud of myself for landing you, when you clearly don't give a shit. You're the one backing away from me like you're afraid of me. *Me*." Myron breathed in through his nose, blowing it out slowly, his face settling into strained lines that made him look unfamiliar. "Fuck, Andy. *You* ambushed *me*, calling me over with barely a clue, looking like I should have understood before you opened the door that we were done." He gestured to where the paper lay. "You even hear yourself just now? *Roger's* neighbor and *Roger's* house. The only thing you got right in all of that was calling Talya your daughter."

"Myron, can't we talk? Are you even hearing me? I want to talk."

"Oh, I heard you. I heard everything. Too much, Andy." He laughed, the sound ragged with pain. "Christ. Looks like I made a fuck of a mistake today."

"What mistake? What did you do?"

"Came out to my boss. My brother. Risked everything for you." Andy's feet moved, taking him towards Myron, and this time it was Myron who held up his hand, palm out, stopping him. *He did that for me.* "Found out I've been stupid there, too. All my life, I've been afraid of losing things that mattered to me. And now—" He swept out a hand as he pulled in a sharp breath, but Andy couldn't tell what he was indicating. "—I got nothing." Myron turned and stomped to the door, yanking it open with a vicious pull. "Nothing here for me."

"Myron," he cried, but the darkness outside the door swallowed up his voice. Then anything else he could have said was drowned by the sound of the motorcycle engine revving. The headlight swung wildly as the bike's back wheel spun dangerously. Then the rubber found traction and Myron was gone.

Soup with sass
Myron

"I don't know what the fuck you want from me." Myron tossed the controller to the table. "Clearly I'm not living up to whatever you need, so why don't you just do it yourself." He turned on his heel and stalked to the door, stopped there by the quiet voice of his friend.

"Brother, stop." Bones' voice held too much of too many things. Compassion, affection, tolerance, and a tiny blade of anger. Myron decided to grab onto that.

"I'm serious. You think it's so easy to do this?" He gestured towards the screen, ignoring the wide-eyed stares from the men seated around the table. "That goddamned drone is in Florida, and I'm here. We don't know what I'm looking for, only that I'm looking for"—he used his fingers to make air quotes—"something out of the ordinary. Well, I'm here to tell you, clue the fuck in, because from where I stand, everything looks out of the ordinary in Florida."

"I think the drone is still flying, and you are the only one of us who can bring it safely back to where it needs to be." Bones stared at him. "It's not like you to quit on us."

"I'm not quitting." As Bones no doubt knew it would, the words goaded Myron into returning to the table and picking up the controller. "And it would go home as soon as the battery got too low." He shook his head sharply. "I'm just frustrated." He yawed the bird, turning it in a circle then pitched it forward to begin flying again.

"As you should be. This is not enough information to warrant a full excursion, and not one of us expects you to find something actionable on a first pass."

"Hold up." Myron spotted something odd on the screen and touched a toggle on the controller, bringing up a secondary instrument window on the screen. "I think..." He flipped to infrared, and a small spot on the display glowed brightly. "That's a hot spot, and that's in the middle of a field of some kind. What do they grow in Florida?"

"I dunno," one of the men said with a laugh. "But, it was a lot of green before you swapped. Are those trees?"

"Christmas trees," Bones agreed, and Myron directed the drone towards the hot spot. He brought it closer, maintaining the current height, then dropped it lower. The spot didn't move, so he dropped it lower yet.

117

The trees could be seen now, ranging thirty feet below in rows off into the distance. Still the spot didn't move. He changed the view back to the camera and heard someone in the room suck in a breath. The person's clothing was stark white against the brown and greens of the dirt and trees, but the red was brilliant and bright. "That is not old blood." Bones shook his head. "I would say that this"—he gestured towards the screen—"is proof that even when you don't know what you're looking for, you seem to find the oddest things."

Myron slipped into that place in his head where he sorted things. Where all things made sense if you only looked at them the right way. Over the next five minutes, he asked questions aloud and waited for responses, then assigned men to different duties such as calling the Jailbreakers MC, their main contacts in the area. Bones called Mason's sister and delicately deduced Justine's safety without flipping her straight into FBI mode, while Myron ran an online search to scour the local PD websites looking for missing persons reports.

Myron fixed the drone at the same height, even though he knew the body lying on the ground in a distant Florida field was dead. From the size, it was a small woman, or a...he just hoped it was a small woman. After a few minutes, Myron had an errant thought and flipped back to infrared, so he could study the screen. "Bones," he called softly, and waited until the man stepped close. "Does it look like the body's cooled in this short time? I thought the heat would be keeping it constant."

"It looks less bright on the screen, yes." Bones nodded.

"If the body is still cooling, then this *just* happened." The drone shot up at his command and he began flying it in larger, concentric circles using the body as a pivot point.

"What is the range on this device?"

"Seven klicks, but I don't trust it. I reset the geofence when I launched, but it could still head home." Myron consulted the clock on the screen. "I've got about twenty minutes left before I have to get it back to the shed." There were drone "sheds" all across the states and Myron was tapped into their network, thanks to Mason shelling out a pretty penny for his access. If there was need and prep time, he could even have a swarm delivered near any specific location, giving him up to ten drones to use.

"What was that?" Bones question corresponded to Myron's movements of the drone, angling towards a grouping of hot spots. "Where are we?"

"About two miles east from the body. There are three men." These bodies were much larger, and their heat wasn't not waning, because they were very much alive. "They're bushwhacking out to the road."

"Fly ahead, see where they are aiming their feet."

Myron ranged out and found a road, then found the little pull-off that was on a straight route back to where he'd seen the men walking. Waiting at that pull-off was another man, and five bikes. "Tell Shades we have a different target for the Jailbreakers. Can you get them this info?" He rattled off the highway information and added, "Tell them they've got less than five minutes and these guys will be wind." He checked the clock again. "Shit, I have about the same before I have to lock GPS so the bird can fly home. Lemme do something." He flipped the drone into hover and moved to the computer. The screen split and within moments, a second view appeared, showing the dim inside of a building. A few seconds passed while his fingers flew across the keyboard, and then the new drone lifted off, turning and yawing for a moment before it oriented on an open door in the ceiling. He watched the screen for a couple of beats, then returned to the controller. "I launched a second, paired it to the original. It'll be onsite in a couple of minutes. That should give us enough time."

"Technology is a strange and marvelous thing."

"It was cool to have Ester video chatting with me the other day." Myron smiled as he backed the drone away, angling to capture the moving images of the men returning to the lone man next to the bikes. "We should see if she'd be open to doing that again."

"Yes, it was cool. What was *not* cool was you upsetting her for no reason." Myron glanced at Bones, seeing tension in his face. "That was not cool at all."

"What do you mean?"

Bones scoffed and shuffled his feet, taking up a stance that looked aggressive, thumbs hooked over the chainlink belt he always wore. "Threatening her with your absence, when you clearly had no such intent. That was not just *not cool*," Bones' head whipped to the side, his angry gaze slicing through Myron, "that was cruel, and not something I expected from you."

"I'm." Myron paused and licked his lips. "I see how it might look that way. I had something happen and decided it would be better to absent myself from the Fort for a few days." He shook his head. "But I am moving. House should be ready to move in by the end of the week. Things are just not...what I had hoped for right now."

He stared at the screen, seeing Andy's face again just before he'd slammed the door, his expression awash with hurt and uncertainty, confusion. Over the past week, Myron had ignored all calls and texts, holding firm through the days and hours until the attempted contacts had dwindled down to nothing. *What if I got it wrong?* The questions plagued him. *It felt so right. Everything did.*

He missed Talya. Missed the little girl with an ever-present ache in his chest. The week he'd spent with them after her release from the hospital had been perfect, like living in a dream. When he thought about Andy, that ache turned to pain. Crushing, grinding him to nothing, the anguish burned in his body all the time. Even here, days later and miles away, standing surrounded by friends and brothers, his throat was tight with the remembered moments spent living...free. Not just out of the closet, but alongside someone who mattered. *Someone I could love.*

"I can't...it's hard to know what to do right now, Bones." He sucked in a hard breath, forcing the wet from his eyes. "I didn't mean to hurt her. She's my sister, man. I love her." *She'd love Talya.* "I just...things are hard right now."

"She will appreciate seeing you tonight for dinner, then. I was uncertain I would extend the invitation, given my anger, but it sounds as if you need family around you." Compassion and understanding blurred the edges of Bones voice, and Myron didn't dare look at him.

Fortunately, he didn't have to, because on the screen, views now synchronized since the second drone had made the trip, they saw a group of bikes approaching on the highway. "Looks like Jailbreakers are headed in. Things are gonna get interesting."

***

"Soup is *too* sassy." Ester's irritation showed in her tone as she refuted a statement from Bones. Myron had to admire the man's willingness to rile her up, but as easy as she made it, clearly the affectionate teasing wasn't something that bothered her.

"How can soup be sassy, Ester? It is merely soup. A meal to be eaten when one needs sustenance." Bones didn't look up, kept his gaze pinned on his bowl where he was casually stirring the steaming liquid with precise movements of his spoon.

"Sass is in the making when you take water and demand it become the more it is in the pot now."

Myron looked down at his own bowl, seeing the noodles and spices floating in the translucent liquid. A wide hunk of homemade bread rested on the edge of a plate nearby, covered in a broad swath of butter.

"Sass is in the air when you breathe it inside, letting the goodness become you." She huffed out a breath in what he understood now was a mock frustration. "That means you have to let the sass out, so the soup is sassy in the end." Not yet done, Ester thudded the butt of her spoon on the table. Myron glanced at her, then at Bones just in time to see the tender look that passed between them. Adoration highlighted the beauty of her features and Ester's face softened as Bones' did the same. Shared jokes, shared lives...shared love.

His gut twisted painfully as any hunger fled. Just that one single look between the two of them that meant everything was something he'd lived his whole life knowing would never be his. Knowing and accepting, telling himself that what he had was good enough. That the brotherhood filled him up in ways that were sufficient, if not satisfactory. It had never been enough, but he'd only known that in the abstract. Now, he knew in his soul how it felt to share a look like that with someone you loved.

I was okay with it once. Myron stared into the soup again, throat tight. *I'll get past this.* He lifted his spoon, and a torrent of drops fell, disturbing the surface of the soup, little ripples racing across the liquid. They slowed and faded, the soup absorbing the energy created by the disturbance. A final droplet clung stubbornly to the edge

123

of the spoon, growing larger as it collected miniscule amounts of soup spread thinly across the metal surface. It clung and clung, resisting the pull of gravity, even though Myron knew it would lose the fight in the end. *Can I really stay away? Don't I deserve to have what Ester and Bones have?* Finally, the droplet fell, and the ending was anticlimactic, ripples ending far sooner than he would have predicted. *Droplet and soup reunited at last.* Myron snorted at his thoughts, dipped the spoon in and lifted it to his mouth.

"Yes, eat, my Ronnie. You deserve some sassy in your life."

I deserved Andy.

***

"You should simply tell me what is wrong, Myron. If you would let it out of your mouth, then someone can help you sort things to the best outcome."

Bones' voice came from behind him. Myron didn't turn, just stared out into the dark garden beyond the kitchen windows. He shook his head and lifted the beer in his hand, drained the bottle and placed it on the table alongside the other three already occupying the space.

"Are you asking me to guess, then? Apply my deducing skills to determine the issue?"

Myron shook his head again. "Couldn't sleep. Found your beer."

Bones laughed. "I am not concerned for the beer." A pause, filled by the scuff of bare foot soles on the floor. "I am concerned for my friend."

"How'd you do it? Convince Ester you were worth the chance? She was so afraid all the time, and then shit happened right outside her bedroom door. Yet, she's still here." Myron shrugged, still staring at the glass but now watching Bones' reflection instead of the dim view of the yard. "How?"

"Is that the crux of the matter for you? Your bartender got a taste of the club and didn't like it?"

"See—" He stood and turned, reseating himself on the chair, arms crossed on the back. "—that's the thing. I don't think he even got a 'taste' as you put it. He read a goddamned article in the paper. It wasn't even about the RWMC, just another club. But he lumped us all in the same boat, and—" He chuckled, the dark sounds ripping his throat raw. "—set fire to that damned thing."

"He cut you loose? No explanation beyond pointing to the newspaper as the bearer of unwelcome tidings?"

"He called me over to talk." Myron scoffed. "Like he wanted to talk. He'd already made up his mind, just needed permission to pull the trigger on breaking what we had." He shook his head. "He never wanted to talk. Just wanted to throw accusations around."

"Are you so certain of that, Myron?" Bones opened the refrigerator and pulled out two bottles, removed the caps and set one in front of Myron. "Or did you do like you sometimes do, as you did today for example, and retreat before understanding what was asked?"

"No, he was done. The conversation was all about 'can you assure me Talya and I are safe?' All of which meant he didn't trust me. Without trust, there can't be...he was just done, Bones. Believe me, I know."

Bones stared down at him, lifted his beer and drank deep, pulling at the bottle for several long swallows. In the shadows, it was hard to know for sure, but it looked like he was scowling. His next words told Myron he'd been right in that assumption. "Allow me a moment to get this straight, if I may. A man you were seeing, who is a single parent to a daughter, and who has already lost one partner in an unexpected event, asked you if his daughter was safe. Myron." Bones shook his head. "He was within his rights to ask that question. The life is not kind to all, and citizens cannot easily understand why we thrive on living outside of the law, yet within the rules binding us together. Especially not if you do not explain *what* we are." He shifted and leaned a hip against the counter. "What is one of the most important things to the Rebels? I know it, and you do too. So tell me, what comes first after the brotherhood?"

"Family." Myron didn't even have to think.

"So why is this man asking you to assure him you would keep his family safe out of line? Why would you consider it an insult, and from the look on your face, it was a grave affront, but why would you not consider the depth of love and trust it took for him to voice the question?" Bones lifted his bottle and drained it, placing it in the bin near the garbage. He turned to pluck the other empties from the table, and took the still full bottle from Myron's hand, upending it over the sink, the amber liquid pouring out in a rush. "You need to ask yourself why you do not trust him."

***

Andy

"Hey, Bex." Andy smiled as Bexley walked towards where he stood at the end of the bar. No, scratch that. She wasn't walking, she was stalking. "What are you drinking tonight?"

"In here? Where my kind aren't welcome? Nothing." Head high, she delivered the blow and watched him with intensity.

"What? What do you mean?" He knew. Myron had talked about their argument, and now Bexley knew. That meant Brute probably knew, too. Other than Myron, Brute was the member he'd bonded with best. They weren't the same, their situations too different to be similar, but he still understood a lot of what drove Brute. Being an oddity, like a scarred combat veteran—or a gay man in a mostly straight town, it was exhausting to be on display all the time.

"You know, the dangerous biker kind? Those bikers who saved me? The ones who make sure hundreds of kids get toys at Christmas, and who paid for the funeral for that homeless veteran last month? The same ones who ride to raise money to combat suicide, and bullying, and cancer? Yeah, those kind. That's what I meant." She flipped her hair, drawing to her full height, her expression furious. "I'm going to take what you said as notice that you don't want us in this bar anymore. I just wanted to come and tell you that you're wrong, and to point out that in my opinion, you've just passed on the chance at probably the best man you could ever have."

She wasn't wrong. He'd known a half a second after opening his mouth that he'd gone about it all the wrong way. "I miss him." Bexley blinked, and Andy realized he'd said that aloud. *In for a penny*, he thought. "Tell me how to make it right."

She stared at him as if daring him to retreat, and Andy stood his ground. *Please, Bex. Help me fix this.*

Slowly, a smile spread across her face, lips curling at the corners as she muttered, "That's more like it."

Give me a tour
Andy

"Who do you think we'll see at the lightning ceremony?"

"Lighting, honey. No lightning tonight." Andy snugged Talya's hat down over her hair and leaned in to kiss her cheek before closing the car door. Once in the driver seat, he settled the radio on a station playing kid versions of Christmas carols, and he and Talya sang along on their way downtown. Tonight was the unveiling of the city's light display, and he had promised her they'd go watch as the giant Santa was illuminated. "I don't know who will be there. Probably some kids from school."

"Will we see Unka Myron?"

Andy's chest compressed as with a blow. *Damn, she can pack a punch.* Mentally he tried to revert to humor as he'd been doing, just getting by. In the weeks since

Myron had walked out, Andy had run the gamut from disbelief to anger, feeling hurt down to his soul, and finally understanding. It killed him, but thanks to Bexley, he thought he finally got it.

What Andy had done was an insult not just to Myron, something his boyfriend would likely have overlooked, but it had been a challenge to Myron's entire way of life. Andy and Bexley had talked far into the night, and with her explanations, he thought he understood. The Rebels weren't a gang, and weren't even the club the newspaper article had been about. Andy had ignorantly lumped them all into the same bucket, kind of like how people did with gay men, when in fact there were as many different varieties in the LGBTQ community as jelly bean flavors. The same was true with motorcycle clubs. Now, he just needed to find a way to get Myron to talk to him again. He'd texted a dozen times, hoping to goad Myron into a response of any kind, only to be met with radio silence that made a profound statement.

"I doubt it, sweetie."

"I miss Unka Myron, Papa."

Me too, honey. He sighed again. *Me, too.* "How many lights do you think they used on Santa?" Diversion tactic number one, because since Myron's explanation of math and statistics—in a six-year-old version, of course—Talya had been enamored of not just counting, that would be a terrible way to generalize her interests, but in projecting answers. Andy had always known she was smart, but her ability to predict some of the things lately was astounding.

"About a hundred million." Her voice was excited, and he laughed. *Astounding, and then she becomes a six-year-old again.*

"I agree." He turned on his blinker, turning into the parking garage. On the second level, he passed a large grouping of motorcycles, lifting a hand when he saw a face he recognized. *Brute.* Heart pounding in his throat, he quickly searched the rest of the group, saddened when Myron wasn't among them. Andy knew Fort Wayne wasn't Myron's home, and thanks to Bexley, he'd found out Myron had been in Chicago for days. He didn't know why he was so disappointed. *Don't be a fool*, he told himself. *You know exactly why.*

They had joined the crowd waiting in the plaza for the countdown to begin when he heard the laugh. He would have known it anywhere, recognized it regardless of the time between the last time he'd heard it and now. Talya heard it, too, and her face turned up to his, joy writ large on her features.

"Unka Myron." Arms lifted, she demanded, "Pick me up, Papa." He did, settling her on his shoulders and within a few seconds knew she'd spotted Myron by the signal of fists beating against the top of his head. "He's here! He's here, Papa."

Andy turned his head at her ungentle directions, the tugging at his hair no match for the terror that had his stomach flipping over in his belly. Would Myron want to see them? *See me?* Across the crowd, he spotted the group of bikers, black leather broken by bright scarves and toboggans, children in poses matching Talya's, riding on broad shoulders. Myron stood to the side, staring up at the unlit display, a smile on his face.

"I wanna see Unka Myron," Talya's cry was imperious, and Andy laughed as her flailing legs escaped his grip, a shoe nearly catching him in the face. "I wanna."

"Okay." *He loves Talya.* Myron would want to see her, even if he didn't give a shit about Andy anymore.

They were about halfway across the plaza when the lights went on. Talya twisted on his shoulders and thumped his head again. "Oh, Papa. It's so beautiful." Myron's head was tipped back, his eyes on the same display, a child's pleasure on his face mirroring the expression Andy knew had to be on Talya's.

"Yeah, it is."

They were within a few yards when one of the bikers caught sight of Andy and called out, "Mouse." That had Myron's head swinging madly from side to side until his gaze latched onto Andy and Talya. Andy froze for a moment, the sudden cessation of movement causing Talya to rock on his shoulders. Then a smile bloomed on Myron's face, starting as a small parting of his lips and building to a beam of joy aimed Andy's way.

"Mouse." Brute stepped in front of him, and the broadness of his shoulders cut off any view of Myron. "Glad to see your little girl's okay."

Andy nodded and stepped to the side as he mouthed his thanks, surprised when Brute moved with him, blocking his path. "Remember what I said when I talked to you at the bar?" Andy's chin jerked back, and he gripped Talya's ankles firmly as he nodded. He did remember, the conversation etched in his head. *"People don't fuck with my friends, or I fuck them back. You hurt mine, I hurt you. Simple as that."* He knew Brute hadn't been exaggerating then, and knew what the man was saying now. "That covers *all* my friends."

"I get it." He held Brute's gaze. "I totally get it."

"Unka Myron, did you see? Papa's here." Talya's flailing had her slipping sideways, and Andy shrugged, trying to straighten her, but Myron pushed around Brute, shoving him to the side with a glare as he reached up, hands catching Talya under her arms. Brute moved away, giving Andy a final scowl over his shoulder.

"Hey, sweetness." Myron pulled her close, and Talya's arms closed around his neck, holding tight. Myron's eyes closed as he kissed the side of her head, and Andy's throat closed at the sight.

"The lights are pretty." She leaned back and twisted again, lifting one hand to point, her finger trembling. "See?"

"Not as pretty as you are, honey." Myron shifted her so she rode one hip, her legs wrapping around his waist. "Are you cold?"

Andy stared, then asked, "Where are your mittens?" *Well, crap.* Her hat was gone, too; lost in the rush to cross the plaza, no doubt.

"I'm cold, Papa." She shivered, not exaggerating the chill, but just cold.

Myron handed her back to Andy, the transfer happening as naturally as if it were something they'd done a thousand times. He gripped Andy's hand for a moment, the strong hold steadying as much as it was thrilling. "Hang on, I got you, honey." He shrugged out of his leather jacket and draped it around her shoulders, tucking the excess around her sides. The Rebel's symbol was sewn to the back of the jacket, and from Andy's perspective, looked as if it were an emblazoned warning, like the club itself would protect her, even if it were only from the cold. That backed up exactly what Bexley had told him. *Why didn't I see it before?* Myron murmured to Talya, "Better?" She nodded, the top of her head knocking against Andy's chin. "How's she doing?" Myron's gaze trailed down then back up, and Andy felt the path of that look like a touch. Then Myron leaned close to kiss Talya's head again, and the scent of him hit Andy's nose, sensory overload pushing him back in time to the last night they'd spent in bed together. Myron's head lifted, and his gaze locked to Andy's, heat filling his eyes. "How are you?"

I'm terrible. Falling apart without you. I want you back, want us back.

He shrugged and swallowed. "Gettin' by." He glanced down to see Talya had one of Myron's hands trapped in hers, holding him close. "She's okay. Wanted to see the lights."

"I missed you." For a long moment, he wasn't certain who had spoken until he saw the light dying in Myron's eyes and realized he was waiting on an answer that Andy hadn't given.

God. "I miss you so much." Hope swirled inside him.

"Talya."

A little girl's cry had his daughter's head lifting. Then she was shouting and wriggling to get down, Myron's coat hanging lopsided from one shoulder. "Gilda!" Myron rescued his jacket as Talya's feet hit the pavement and she darted through the adults, meeting another little girl with an enthusiastic hug. "Papa, look it's Gilda."

Another biker stooped next to the two girls, grinning broadly. "You must be the Talya Gilda keeps wanting to adopt. She said you're the best imaginer in class. Jumped ahead a grade, right?" Talya nodded, still swinging her friend back and forth. The biker stood and looked at Andy, then did a doubletake. "Mouse, how are ya, man?" It was Captain, one of the bikers who had stood sentry for Bexley. They'd had dozens of interesting conversations. The man was a retired professional athlete, and had turned that passion for his sport into a way to give back to the community, running a program for underprivileged youth. Andy had looked it up, and convinced the bar owners to donate to it this Christmas. *It's been in front of me all along.*

"I'm fine. Hey, it's good to see you." Captain's vigorous handshake pushed him to the side, and Andy bumped into Myron. Five circles of heat hit his back, and he realized Myron had steadied him. Every atom of his being wanted to lean into that pressure, but he held himself upright. "Gilda's your daughter?" Continued pressure on his spine told him Myron hadn't moved away, hadn't dropped his hand, and while Andy knew what he wanted to make of that fact, he still wasn't certain what it meant.

"Yeah, one of 'em. I have—" Captain's mouth quirked. "—a few." He looked at Myron. "How're your decorations coming, brother? That new house is too big for one guy. I think," he winked at Andy, "you need a little girl or two to fill that space." Captain rocked back on his heels following that startling pronouncement and shook his head. "But, just not tonight." Gilda and Talya were dancing in circles between the men, chins tipped up as they sang a Christmas song Talya had learned in the car tonight. "I think tonight Talya needs to come watch a movie with my girls."

"Papa, may I?"

Ignoring Talya's pleading eyes, Andy turned to Myron. "You bought a house?" Myron nodded, his expression cautious. "In Fort Wayne?" Another nod. "Where? Why?"

Myron took a breath, then murmured softly, "Up off Bethel."

Andy gawked. "That's near Talya's school. Near me." He licked his lips, and Myron's gaze fell to his mouth, staying there as he nodded a third time. "Why?"

"I wanted—"

"Papa, I want to go to Gilda's. Her momma says it's okay. Can I?" Talya pushed between them, staring up. "Please? Papa? Unka Myron? Can I?"

Andy looked up from Talya's face when he felt Myron's fingers spasm at his waist. He was still staring down at Talya, his mouth soft, a look of surprise on his features. *Probably didn't expect her to enlist him in her pleas.* Andy knew what he had to do, knew he had to be the one to move them back to where they needed to be. "Hey." He kept his voice soft, waiting for Myron to look up. "I wanna see that house. If she goes for a movie, you can take me there." He grinned, and Myron looked at his mouth again. "You know, give me a tour. Show me around. I think I'd like that."

"I'd like that, too."

Falling for you
Myron

Myron straddled the seat of his bike, watching as the car crept towards him, Andy waving from the front seat. He pulled out of the parking spot, the vehicle following closely as they made their way to the street and then aimed west and north. Nearly the route Andy would take to go home, but a world away from where they'd been before.

This was it, what he'd been hoping for when he had the first conversation with the real estate agent weeks ago. If he had his wish, Andy would be riding behind him, because hadn't that night been a revelation. Having Andy on the seat behind him had made him feel ten feet tall, and it hadn't taken but a moment before he'd understood the draw for his fellow bikers. Having someone you were interested in wrapped around you, that was just impossibly arousing. Myron grinned as he leaned the bike through a corner, eyes flicking to the car behind him. Should have been a foreshadowing of how they'd sleep together, because it didn't matter how they'd fallen asleep, Andy had wound himself around Myron.

Probably why my sleep's been shit. Since he'd walked away—he knew there would be groveling in his future, but right now he wasn't giving a fuck about that— he'd been lucky to piece together four or five hours sleep a night, troubled rest only coming in fits and starts.

He didn't expect to see Andy tonight, or Talya. In fact, he hadn't known where they were headed, just pulled up at the clubhouse as the big group was readying to leave, cars full of kids following. Talya knowing Jase's littlest was pure luck, too.

He rounded the final turn and glided up the driveway to the house, slowing so the garage door could open completely. Myron had scarcely gotten parked and dismounted before Andy was right there, hand on his arm, eyes wide in his face.

"Oh my God, it's gorgeous. This is yours?" Myron nodded. "Show me."

"Not just yet." Andy frowned, and then when Myron leaned in, a look of comprehension dawned on his features, eyes becoming heavy-lidded as Myron kissed him like he'd wanted to at the plaza. With his friends around, in the middle of a crowd, uncaring of who saw or might give a shit. The only reason he hadn't was fear. Not of what people might say, since between the responses of Mason, Bones, and Slate, he'd been relieved from that fear. No, he was terrified Andy wouldn't want it, wouldn't want him. Wouldn't give him this chance to make everything right. *I want to explain everything.*

Myron tried to tell him all that and more through the play of lips and tongue, going from gentle caresses to a deeper, more thorough exploration of Andy's mouth. Tongues touching tentatively, then rubbing together like velvet, Myron played with his mouth, trying to force every emotion he'd suppressed over these past days. Telling Andy only that he'd missed him felt as if it'd minimized the depth of longing he'd felt every breath, and he tried to press the truth into the kiss. Longing and desire, fear, the feeling of coming home that was Andy's hands at his neck. Myron gave everything to Andy, and he realized in the middle of it all, that Andy was giving it right back to him.

Myron broke the kiss finally, and shoved his face into Andy's neck and wrapped his arms around tightly, appreciating the firm planes of muscles beneath his hands.

"Jesus, My." Andy's breath came quick, mixed with a little groan. "I missed you."

"Backatcha." He pulled in air for a final sigh, then pulled back, relaxing his hold. "I want to tell you about this, what I did."

Andy's lips stretched, curving up at the ends, the center bowing down in that way Myron found too tempting. "I know what you did, babe. You—" He leaned in, heat from his lips drifting across Myron's jaw. "—bought a house for us."

"I did." He admitted it straight out, not holding anything back. "I listened to you, even when I wasn't doing so good at communicating, I was listening. I heard you."

"I heard you, too. I want you to know that." Andy grinned and touched his forehead to Myron's, mouth so close every breath mingled. "I want us to be okay. I want you." His hand slipped down Myron's arm, fingers threading through and squeezing. Andy sounded certain when he commanded, "So, why don't you show me what you did." Myron let the certainty he'd felt when he first looked at the house give him courage, and he nodded, excitement and anticipation of what Andy would think making him rush to open the door.

They moved through the house, Andy exclaiming loudly about all the things Myron had imagined he would, his excitement contagious. Walking hand-in-hand, his dream of living there together no longer seemed so impossible; it was reality in the making. At the door to Talya's room, Andy just stood for the longest time, quiet. He still looked relaxed, but Myron had no idea what was going through his head. Finally, he turned and tilted his face to look into Myron's eyes. They were wet, swimming with tears, and Myron cupped the sides of his neck, pulling him close. "What?"

"She's gonna love it." Andy offered him a shaky smile. "She really is."

"And you?" *Please, tell me you love it. Tell me you understand what I'm saying.*

"I love you. I don't care where we are, as long as we're together." Myron froze, those words not at all what he'd been expecting. Hoping, sure, but expecting? No way. "I know you'll say it's too soon, or there's too much we need to talk about. That we need to be sure. But, My. I *am* sure."

"Falling for you, too. Tried to not, mostly because of how twisted up I was in my head. But I think I'm falling, Andy." He smiled, feeling his lips tremble. "I am. I did." Myron buried his face against Andy's shoulder, and while fabric muffled his last declaration, he knew Andy heard him. "I do."

Not even a Mouse

Andy, one year later

"Hallo, the house."

The shout echoed through the rooms, and Andy sat up, sheets puddling in his lap as Myron rolled to the edge of the bed and stood. Andy took a moment to admire that fine, round ass as it disappeared into jeans, and then he looked up, caught Myron's broad, indulgent smile and returned it.

Giggles wound up the hallway, and Andy barely had time to exit the bed and pull his own pants on before Talya came barreling around the doorframe. Gilda, still their girl's best friend, was right behind her, and both girls flopped onto the comforter still billowing down from Myron's quick toss.

"I wanna do this every year, Papa." She reached out her hand and grabbed his finger, squeezing tight. "Christmas Eve Eve at Miss DeeDee's is fun."

As they had last year, Jase and DeeDee had offered to take Talya for an evening, letting Andy and Myron celebrate in peace and quiet. Now it was Christmas Eve, and she was back home.

"Y'all decent in there?" Threaded with quiet humor, the question came from the hallway, and Myron snorted a laugh. Jase's head popped into view around the door and he grinned. "Just checkin'. Don't need to see no twigs and berries, eh?"

"Jesus." Myron's groan made Talya laugh, which made Gilda laugh, which in turn made Jase laugh.

Andy grinned.

"Papa?" He angled his neck to look down at his little girl who was looking back up at him, uncertainty on her face. At seven, she was more articulate and composed than a lot of little girls, but being raised by two men who made no bones about the fact they loved her gave her a lot of courage. She was willing to try anything once, including horseback riding—a flop—and ice skating—a huge win. She'd found she loved the sport. After watching her first time lacing up and declaring her a natural, Jase hadn't wasted any time slotting her into his skating groups at his foundation. Gilda preferred to watch from the sidelines while Talya bounced from ice to her blades, and then back to her tush on the ice, but their little girls were fast friends, never far from the other.

144

"Yeah, baby?" He grabbed a shirt from the dresser and tugged it on, tucking it into his jeans around his waist.

"When I grow up, I want to kiss girls." Andy had been looking at Myron, and so was treated to the sight of his eyes going wide in shock.

"Me, too. I wanna kiss girls, too." Gilda's input did nothing to lesson Myron's look of frozen fear.

"*And* boys. I wanna kiss girls and boys," Talya declared with more certainty in her tone.

Jase rescued both of them with a quick, "If you wanna kiss the girls, that's okay. Or the boys. You can kiss who you want. But not this year. And not even the next, eh? No, for you two troublemakers, kissin' is definitely gonna hafta wait 'til you're both at least fifteen. Minimum kissin' age. No arguments. Do what you want, but not until we say so." Jase maneuvered Myron until he stood at the foot of the bed and turned him, poking and pulling until Myron's arms swung out to the sides. "Now, you needa move, or Unka Myron's gonna squish you. He's gonna timber on a count of three. One."

"Two." The girls squealed and rolled to the sides, then finished the count. "Three."

Jase pushed, and Myron fell backwards amid little girl giggles and an astonishing amount of male chuckles, and Andy shook his head. "You okay, babe?"

Before Myron could answer, Talya's voice trilled out another question, this one making Andy stop in his tracks. "Papa, do we still hang a stocking for Daddy?" Last year, their final one celebrated in Roger's home, Andy had hung the three stockings as they had every year.

"Do you want to, baby?" He looked at her, loving how protectively Myron's arm curled around her.

Her little head shook back and forth slowly. "Not this year. I wanna put up a stocking for...Papa Myron." After dropping that bomb, she chewed on her lip for a moment and then asked, "Is that okay?"

Andy thought of the present he had tucked in his drawer for Myron, and grinned. "Yeah, I think that'd be perfect."

***

Myron

"She's going to be up early." Andy's muffled voice came from behind him. They were squeezed together on the couch, a place that was Myron's favorite place to snuggle. *Well, except for in bed.* He grinned, eyes closed, ignoring the decades-old Christmas movie playing on the TV.

"She is," he agreed, edging backwards with his hips, rewarded by a groan and a thrust against his ass. "Lookie there. You're up right now."

"I am." Andy placed a kiss on the back of his neck, and Myron twisted around, meeting his mouth for a tender kiss. "However, it's Christmas Eve, which means uncertain sleeping patterns. She might be dead to the world right now, but that can change at any moment." Andy kissed him again, possessing his mouth like Myron loved him to, pushing the kiss farther before he slowed things back down. "Which means we need to lock the door."

"We can do that. Promise you we'll hear her squealing about the tree long before she gets to our bedroom, though." Myron stopped and took a breath, thinking to himself again how astonishing his life had become. *Our bedroom.* Andy kissed him again, stealing all thoughts from his head, leaving him panting and rocking his hips against the couch cushion, trying for any friction against his rigid cock. "Jesus, Andy. You're killing me here."

"I have something for you." Andy's voice was soft, and Myron chuckled, pushing his hips back. "Not that." Andy showed his words a lie as he pressed forwards, rubbing and thrusting. "I mean, yeah, this is yours."

"You know it." Myron's mutter was joking, and Andy knew it. There was no jealousy between them, no worry that the other would stray or might look for variety. They'd only been together a year, but they both knew it was for keeps.

"I have a present for you. I was going to wait until tomorrow, but now..." Another touch of his lips to Myron's. "I wanna give it to you now."

"I have something for you, too." Myron rolled off the couch and bent, fumbling to open the coffee table drawer. Present in hand, he turned to find the couch was empty and twisted to see Andy headed down the hallway to their room. Instead of climbing back on the couch, he pulled a folded blanket off a nearby chair and settled on it with his back against the couch. Myron watched Andy walk back into the room, holding a manila envelope that looked suspiciously like the one in his hands.

"What did you do?" Andy folded himself to sit next to Myron, studying both envelopes.

"I think the question is what did you do?" They sat like that for a moment, then both men burst out into laughter, each shushing the other. Myron leaned forwards and plucked the envelope from Andy's hands, replacing it with the one he'd prepared. "Take turns or same time?"

Andy stared at him without speaking, and finally whispered, "Same time."

Myron nodded. "On three."

Andy nodded. "One. Two."

They both said, "Three," and Myron was chuckling as he bent the tines back, opening the envelope and shaking the contents into his hands. A quick review had his heart stuttering in his chest, and he looked to see Andy staring at him, papers clutched in his grip, fingers white with force of his hold.

"You want this?" Andy's question was a whisper, awe in his voice. Myron nodded.

"Yours is better," Myron told him, and Andy shook his head. "Gimme a pen, right now." Andy produced one from the pocket of his jeans, and Myron scribbled his signature. "They're both awesome."

"They are."

Myron looked down at the papers he held, a summary judgment that, once he signed it, had made him an adoptive parent of one Natalya Lyons-Kasmouski.

The name choice was fortunate, because the papers Andy held officially changed Myron's government name to Ronald Lyons-Kasmouski. Better known as Myron, which was short for My Ronnie.

"Race you to bed?"

It was only fitting that Andy made it to their bedroom first, Myron close behind him. When Andy had learned his name, they had both laughed, because what was more appropriate than for a cat to catch a mouse. A few hours later, the air rang with Talya's happy shouts, but in the time between them falling asleep holding each other, exhausted and boneless, and Talya's thudding wakeup call on their locked door, their home was quiet.

Nothing stirring.

Not even a Mouse.

THANK YOU FOR READING
Not Even A Mouse!

ABOUT THE AUTHOR

Raised in the south, MariaLisa learned about the magic of books at an early age. Every summer, she would spend hours in the local library, devouring books of every genre. Self-described as a book-a-holic, she says "I've always loved to read, but then I discovered writing, and found I adored that, too. For reading...if nothing else is available, I've been known to read the back of the cereal box."

Also by MariaLisa deMora

Alace Sweets

A dark thriller, this book is not a light read. Filled with edge-of-your-seat suspense, this intense story commands the reader's attention as it drives towards the explosive ending. Alace Sweets is a vigilante serial killer, with everything that implies and is sure to trip all your triggers. Be ready.

At seventeen, Alace Sweets turned a corner in her life, taking the wrong shortcut home from school.

Resisting the harsh knowledge her attackers will never be made to pay for their actions, Alace takes a stand. Justice must be served, and if fate's scales are out of balance, she's determined to set things right as best she can.

When the laws of men fail, the rules of Alace prevail.

5-Star Reviews for Alace Sweets

"deMora has a superb story-line and exceptional character development. All of her characters have such depth that will intrigue the reader..."
~Turning Another Page

"Hot, sweet, dark thriller."
~Beth D

"It will keep you on the edge of your seat and give you chills."

~Manda M

"This book takes you a dark and twisted ride that is gripping..."
~Renee Entress' Blog

"This book is dark and gritty and I literally had to take a day off from reading it because it's that intense."
~My Girlfriend's Couch

"This is my favourite book so far from this author ... I recommend this book if you enjoy dark romantic thrillers."
~Cheekypee Reads and Reviews

"There's not enough stars to give this book and 5 just doesn't really do it justice!"
~DeLane C

"I couldn't put this book down from page one! Tried to stop & go to bed but couldn't sleep thinking about Alace and got up & finished the book."
~Debbie M

"MariaLisa DeMora, wordsmith that she is, made this a story of the enlightenment of a woman and finding love in a life where she has had none."
~Kat W

"Whatever deep dark trench [deMora] pulled a character like Alace from should be revisited again and often."
~Confessions of a Serial Reader

ADDITIONAL SERIES AND BOOKS

Please note that books in a series frequently feature characters from additional books within that series. If series books are read out of order, readers will twig to spoilers for the other books, so going back to read the skipped titles won't have the same angsty reveals.

Rebel Wayfarers MC series:

Mica, #1
A Sweet & Merry Christmas, short story #1.5
Slate, #2
Bear, #3
Jase, #4
Gunny, #5
Mason, #6
Hoss, #7
Harddrive Holidays, short story #7.5
Duck, #8
Biker Chick Campout, short story #8.5
Watcher, #9
A Kiss to Keep You, novella #9.25
Gun Totin' Annie, short story #9.5
Secret Santa, short story #9.75
Bones, #10
Gunny's Pups, novella #10.25
Never Settle, short story #10.5
Not Even A Mouse, short story #10.75
Fury, #11
Christmas Doings, #11.25
Gypsy's Lady, #11.5
Cassie, #12
Road Runner's Ride, novella #12.5

Occupy Yourself band series:

Born Into Trouble, #1
Grace In Motion, #2 (TBD)
What They Say, #3 (TBD)

Neither This, Nor That series:

This Is the Route Of Twisted Pain, #1
Treading the Traitor's Path: Out Bad, #2
Trapped by Fate on Reckless Roads, #3 (TBD)

Other Books:

With My Whole Heart
Alace Sweets
Hard Focus

More information available at mldemora.com.

www.ingramcontent.com/pod-product-compliance
Lightning Source LLC
Chambersburg PA
CBHW061238170626
46809CB00007B/2727